Chuck Kruger, born 1938, grew up
traipsing around old Iroquois hunting and burial grounds. Educated, in addition, at Hamilton College (AB), Bread Loaf School of English, Washington University (MA), the C. G. Jung Institute, Zürich. His adult life has seen him move from secondary school teacher of lit., phil., psych., & the humanities to denizen of an Irish island, where he writes every morning, prowls cliff & cave & rabbit track every afternoon. He has read many of his pieces on RTE's "Sunday Miscellany" and "Seascapes", on Lyric FM's "Quiet Quarter", and on the USA's "Weather Notebook" (National Public Radio); co-edited *Shadow and Evil in Fairy Tales* (Spring Publications, 1974); wrote *Cape Clear: Island Magic* (Collins Press, 1994, '95, '99), an international thriller *The Man Who Talks To Himself* (Southernmost House Press, 1998), and his first collection of short stories, *Flotsam & Jetsam* (Bradshaw Books, 2000). Of his adopted island Chuck says: "Cape's a poem I read every day, every night. It's a point of reference, a metaphor by which I confirm my very being. It's the place I love more than any other."

Between a Rock

CHUCK KRUGER

bradshaw books
Cork, Ireland

First published in 2004 by

bradshaw books
Tigh Filí (Poets' House)
Thompson House
MacCurtain Street
Cork, Ireland
Phone (353) 21 450 9274
Fax (353) 21 455 1617
Website www.tighfili.com

British Library Cataloguing in Publication Data

ISBN 0 949410 98 7

Book design by Nick Sanquest
Cover photograph by the author
Printed and bound by Colourbooks, Dublin

ACKNOWLEDGMENTS

Special thanks to the Bryan MacMahon Short Story Competition 2003 (part of the Listowel Writers' Week Festival), which awarded "Hard Place" first prize; to *The Dubliner* short story contest '02, which awarded "Calling" its first prize; to the *Cork Literary Review's* 2000 & 1998 short story competitions, which awarded "Gas Man" and "Click, Click" first prizes, and "Temper, Temper" second prize in 1999; to the *Francis MacManus* short story contests of 2001 and 2002 which shortlisted "Worm of the Sea" and "Boundaries, Bulls, and Brendans"; and to the *Bealtaine Laois Literature Festival* 2003 for awarding "King Conger" its second of two prizes. Also thanks to David Marcus, who published "Belated Rite of Passage" in *Phoenix Irish Short Stories* 1999.

Dedicated to Nell,

Co-Editor of My Life,

And to Our First Issues, Charles, Meredith, & Nathaniel,

And – Whoopee! – to Theirs

CONTENTS

Hard Place

Cuddy'd heard how the vertical joints were weeping, how the bolts were wasted, dripping rust like blood. But he'd never seen the actual Fastnet Lighthouse until now. With less than a rutted mile to go before reaching the mainland site called Rock Island, he stuck his head out the window, called the carriage to a halt. There, southeast of Spanish Point, rose the tower. Eight miles out to sea, a ring of pulsing white around its craggy base, the principal lighthouse off Ireland's southwest coast stood serene. Yet he sensed not peace but challenge.

Suddenly a thought crossed his mind like an arrow: he was about to experience what it's like to become an adult orphan. "Out there," it zinged, "you're cut off from all you've ever known."

Thunk.

While trying to extract its barb, he read the message the arrow carried: "Out there, the natural mothering and fathering rhythms of life are absent utterly; out there, you're imprisoned, though, for a change, on a reliable salary."

Zang.

"Right so!" he called to the driver.

Whip snapped against flank. Carriage jolted. Ridge of bracken, gorse, and old red sandstone blocked seascape.

Arriving at Rock Island pier and stopping under the gantry, Cuddy may not yet have known a Beaufort 11 from a zephyr, a rogue wave from a confidence man, but he knew granite, that most durable of building-stones: how to set it, fit it, mix the mightiest mortar, achieve the sturdiest of joins. He could tell at a glance that from Cornwall, Devon, Dublin, Peterhead; knew not only how to grout, but when.

First strength; later, looks.

Toward the slipway pier powered four men, an oar each. Cuddy dropped the loop of tossed bow rope around a designated bollard.

"'Tis the calm before the storm, lads. In with ye," called the man in the stern, "'cause we've to take you in and hie ourselves back to Crook 'fore dark. 'Twouldn't want no Big Wind the likes of '39 to turn us into no kite. All aboard."

Next Cuddy knew, perched on the bow thwart, his three workmen astern, he became aware that, even without wind, the sea had a way of breathing, of lifting them up and up as if to the knoll of a hill, and then of lowering them down and down, as if into a lonely valley from which nothing could be seen save wave and sky.

"My barometer, she's dropped from the 'a' in fair to the 't' in storm as of noon," said the oarsman closest to Cuddy. "No crisis. But worrying. The sooner we make this crossing, and the return – nigh on sixteen miles – the sooner Mr MacMahon declares bankruptcy."

"Mr MacMahon?"

"Our local undertaker."

"Oh," laughed Cuddy.

The swells, some sixty feet wide from trough to trough, may have been old and lazy, but they communicated to Cuddy a relaxed power that–

"Wave coming! Turn starboard fifteen degrees! Straight into her so."

The shout brought him back. The sudden veering of the boat. The scramble in the stern.

As they rose, he surveyed his human matchstick lack of worth. And they rose and rose until he felt as if they were in the air, gliding like a gull. And then they were descending, diving, sliding-skidding down the back of the wave, a bow wave exploding beside him.

The stern oarsman, who'd changed the position of his blade so that it now jutted out like a rudder from a notch in the transom, had both arms wrapped about his oar.

And they were back on course, the Fastnet dead ahead.

As they closed the final hundred-yard stretch, Cuddy became aware of a steady roar from the southeastern swells washing around the foot of the Rock. The tower loomed. It seemed as if that the world had been condensed into surrounding sea, tower, Rock.

The workers on the Rock prepared the landing crane, swinging it out over the middle of the eighty-foot-wide inlet to the northeast of the island. A rope basket depended from a cable.

"We hold the *St. Ciarán* in the middle of this cove," explained the skipper, "and you lads scramble aboard the basket. We'll toss you your luggage and reach you your toolboxes once you've nested. Yes, they'll direct the basket alongside, careful that it don't snag on no oars or spurs. And look out for them waves so. What gave us a push out there wasn't but a sprat. Here you need be on your lookout for sharks. Cheers, lads. Good keeping. God bless!"

With the *St. Ciarán* rising and falling, on average, some nine feet in the swells, every time its gunwale reached the circumference level of the basket, one of the men leapt into it, then prepared to assure the safety of the next. Cuddy, at thirty-three the oldest of the masons, went first, Robert last. Shortly Cuddy and Dineen lay down in the net, shoulders at the edge, and snatched their belongings from the skipper over the next five ascents.

"Clockwork," cried the skipper, as he saluted the gantry operator, the signal to swing the men onto the Rock.

"Safe home," shouted Cuddy, as he felt the basket start its swoop.

In less than a minute they were lowered onto the landing ledge. Cuddy disentangled himself from the net. When he looked up, the foreman of the entire workforce, which now numbered twelve, stood beside him. They shook hands. "Welcome," Wayne smiled somewhat formally. "Welcome to the last place God made. You're Cuddy? Good man. Michael here will show you your quarters. It's military, three to a bed these Boer War days. But lying spoonways makes it easier. Why, as a boy my parents once put me down to lie between two cows – no better warmth, they said."

"We're bulls, sir," said Dineen.

"No bother, son," Wayne acknowledged with a grin. "Dinner's at 6:00 sharp. In half an hour," he said, after pulling a watch out of his fob pocket. "And work begins tomorrow at 5:00. You'll be wakened." He tucked tie back under waistcoat.

The next morning, with the lighthouse barometer reassuringly up, Cuddy observed intently as the crew of the *Ierne*, moored to the northeast by three permanent anchors off the starboard side and two island bollards off the port, secured the hook of the island's major crane to a carefully wrapped three-ton granite ashlar and pushed the block along rollers to the ship's side, tumbled it into sea. Once the block had sunk straight down from the extended hoist's tip, a Rock worker shifted the motorised steam landing-winch into gear and began raising the heaviest block in the fifty-year history of the Fastnet to the surface and, dripping, on up.

Trundled along the short precipitous track over to the site, the ashlar was next lifted and lowered by yet another crane, with a short setting-jib, toward its long-planned position. Cuddy, designating where the stone should be set so that the next stone could dovetail with it, knew that he knew the parameters, but found that he alone had to stand directly beneath the descending stone to oversee – or, as he put it, undersee – its exact journey. This stone, like all coming after it, had to be perfectly aligned; he couldn't permit a 1/32 of an inch error, else the entire structure could go off its axis. The vertical ellipse line, he knew, started now.

While proud to be so intimately involved, Cuddy also abruptly realised that he alone of all workers was at risk. Were any rope, chain, or cable to break, that block would come down on the father of his children. Squash. No arguing with ashlars.

As he ran his hands along the arrises, he tried to push aside the thought that if he was already in prison, this new realisation relegated him to solitary confinement. He shook his head abruptly in a physical attempt to cast off the recognition. After all, he'd a wet dark bed of Portland cement ready to welcome his potential murderer.

As the block came even with him, he directed it carefully into place, his caressing hands checking every edge and making final adjustments. He nodded his men forward. They removed the ropes, chains, and protective boards, trowelled off the ooze of cement – and waited for the next block, one to be fitted to this one, every block from now on, he interpolated, fitted to every neighbouring block, male and female created He them, this my Eden and me and my caressing hands . . . without my Eve.

Joan, soul mate, bedmate, mother to our four boys and daughter, I vow I'll write you every day – and eat every apple you send.

But my love, how'd I get to where three-ton blocks dangle overhead? If Fate, then there's that thread of fate. Cable. Damocles. No, Cuddy, look not up but around: that speck of mainland resplendent in shaft of light, the seas around the Rock washing by on good behaviour, not a wave yet today from half tide on down within ten feet of me – but, yes, always the thought of that wave, that storm, that–

A shiver coursed through his body. His ellipse line teetered. Joan vanished.

He climbed to the tramway where his men were observing the offloading of the *Ierne*.

"Now, lads, the fun begins. This one's not only got to have a welcoming wet bed, and side, but welcoming wet joins. That means it's got to be lowered absolutely level – and our joins, and our grouting, begin in earnest. Let's get back down there, have everything ready for the next guest."

"Guest?"

"Potential assassin."

"Now you're talking, boss. He's all yours."

Directly under the second ashlar, Cuddy again gave hand signals to the crane operator as the stone was lowered. It not only had to be perfectly level, but exactly parallel with the first stone so that the dovetailing could take place without snapping any edges. Additional guide ropes kept the stone from swinging. When lowered to half an inch higher and to the southeast side of the first stone, Cuddy signalled stop, studied fall lines, reconnoitred. He and his men removed the protective wooden slats from the new stone's edges. Cuddy signalled for the quarter-inch by quarter-inch final lowering. When the stone had settled snugly into place, he noticed his breaths came no faster than at the start of the operation.

But as he and his men started trowelling, the main landing-derrick cable developed a kink just below the top pulley. The *Ierne*, informed that it would be unable to offload any more stone that day until a new cable was installed, returned to Rock Island two-thirds full.

Consequently, after an hour spent making certain that the joins had not a discernible bubble left in them before grouting all visible seams and rechecking the foundation bed for the rest of the first course, Cuddy set out to explore the tower.

He climbed up and round and round the spiralling stairs to the lantern. The keeper on duty, John O'Driscoll from Youghal, welcomed him, gave him a tour. After introductions, chat about the weather, worms of the sea, how some people could never learn to spot tidal movement, nor discern right off a frigate on the horizon, Cuddy chanced his questions.

"Have you family?"

"Yes."

"How do you survive without being with them?"

"Ah, when I get my week off, they're there, right over there, in Crook, in newly-built housing for us keepers."

"But you can't make up for all the time away."

"That's good, Cuddy. I try to do something special with each offspring every time I'm out. Something with the missus too. And with the whole bunch together. A walk. A meal out in Goleen. A pony ride thanks to my neighbour Bernie. Something with each of them and with all of them I've never done before. All seven of us. That more than makes up for this isolation. Sweet Jesus Mary and Joseph but I see more of them in that week off than I would had I been working at a nearby mainland job."

"'When you're not fishing be mending the nets.' Thanks, Johnny. Gives perspective. But tell me, have you ever been, well, terrorised out here?"

"Ha. Once. Two winters back. December 29th. Me and Matt on day duty, Tim on the eight-hour night shift. I'm asleep, wake to hear the whole structure screaming. And then all quiet, quiet as inside a womb. For twenty seconds or so. Then the scream again. And I mean scream. I'm confused, can't wait for the bliss, the utter peace, to return. Matt, in the bed beside me, he's awake too. We daren't budge. Oh, those moments of quiet, how we cherish 'em. And then, after half an hour of nightmare, half an hour that seems forever, and then some, all's back to normal. Well, yes, massive waves we hear breaking. But no screaming, no eerie bliss. In the morning Tim gives a detailed blow-by-blow account of what happened. Wave after wave, not just crest after crest, went over the tower. The scream was the wave coming, the swirling spray in front of it whistling through ropes and cables, and the peace the wave placing the tower under water, placing us back in mum's womb. Tim couldn't leave the lantern. Said he froze in place at the horror he saw, most the seas' tops over the bottoms of his windows, the rest of the tower submerged. But only once, Cuddy, once like that in my eleven years here. Oh, sure, waves every winter break over the tower, but that's their crests, not their bulk, mere foam and froth and sea spit. Ninety-foot-high waves. Now you know what not to become."

"A keeper."

"A keeper."

"You've got me wondering."

"'The quickest road's the road your mind's set on.' Some people's senses come and go with the moon. Here you need be steady on, no matter wind or wave or spring tides. What think you?"

"I think I'm not thinking, Johnny, but orienting myself. Something about this place that feels utterly alien, a tower of tears – yet utterly home. I've some sorting out to do. My own ellipse line's off centre."

"Credit to ye. Most wouldn't admit what you've just said. Sweet Jesus but if we all liked the same thing, wouldn't we be one boring bunch!"

"Johnny, you're my mentor. I'm back to the lads."

"Any time, my friend."

They shook hands.

When he exited the front door of the tower, Cuddy walked across a flat area, stopped at a railing. Far below, straight beneath him, he noticed a bevy of grey Atlantic seals, some sunning themselves, others simply playing in the jade green water. He felt included, privileged, an adult orphan no more.

Not until the 13th of June did the Fastnet receive more ashlars. On this day Cuddy and his men were able to complete the first course and start the second. By the end of August the partial ring-courses were set, stepped, grouted, and course 14 underway. And as the last of the 73 stones for this course was being lowered, with Cuddy in his usual position, he saw above him, instead of a crane lowering granite, some mythological bird, a prehistoric pelican, and himself about to become but a tidbit in its bill, something to be snatched, chewed, digested, excreted. But aren't we all in a similar state, he speculated; no matter where we are we're dependent for our very lives on matters beyond our control. Lightning. War. Falling off a ladder, off a cliff, off a course. Off course. Ellipse line gone. Always, yes, above us – below us – in us – some monster that might gobble us up, snuff out our lives as easily as I make a motion with my trowel. But being so visibly, tangibly near death, is that any different from what all of us are, any time, any place, not just on the Fastnet under a three-ton block that may or may not have our names on it? Death's always lurking, boy. Back in June, that first monster over me, I felt death's breath. Now, this monster's more a curiosity – and the situation makes me more alive, helps me feel an intensification of life. Thank you, bird of death.

Wayne called for a five-minute break.

And Cuddy climbed back to rail, this time saw not seals but a motionless grey heron, which suddenly, from its low perch on a rock, stabbed a fish, swallowed it down with head thrown back. Cuddy blinked at this way of life on the Fastnet, this intensity of connection to a minute world. Perhaps that which he'd perceived as a threat of death was but a quickener, a force that when properly absorbed gave him more life, more sense of life. Joan, I'm ready.

Yes – he saw as if the Fastnet light itself were focused on a dangerous rock, warning off all passing ships – the assurance of death makes life worth living. If no death, life – even Joan – would lose all value. You wouldn't need a Fastnet; wouldn't need a stronger tower, a brighter light. What could be more boring than a flower forever in bloom? Well, except for gorse, you eejit.

Wayne called out. Work resumed. Cuddy finished guiding granite into place.

On the 2nd of September Cuddy and crew completed their best work of the season, setting twenty-two stones in one day. By the end of the month they'd set a summer total of 268 blocks before the weather broke and it was time to return to the mainland.

But by then, looking 360 degrees around him, Cuddy knew as surely as he knew his own callused hands – hands that had felt every inch of every sharp arris of every block laid to date – what he wanted to do with the rest of his working life. And where. Joan was for it, and for moving to Crook. And Johnny'd agreed to write his reference.

Boundaries, Bulls, and Brendans

Boundaries confuse me. Don't know where I begin any more than where I'll end. How many generations back need I go to establish bona fide roots? Two? Five? Five thousand? Date of birth, of death, one thing, genes another, influence of inherited island environment yet another. What happens when being a would-be dutiful but won't-be subservient wife, or a mother at any hour of need or no-need, or a helpful but not-to-be-run-over neighbour, or a voracious but not sweetly vegetarian reader, or a frankly female farmer, conflicts with being ruddy me? Why, I don't even know where my farm – my country, so to speak – begins and ends. Physically, yes, I can walk the walls, read the ordnance survey map, agree categorically with the coastline. But morally? What responsibility do I bear for toxic weeds – let alone the Sellafields – that spread from my townland to a neighbour's? How can I justify owning a hundred and twenty acres with house and sheds when dispossessed children by the millions haven't a bed to cuddle up in, let alone a mother to hug? Slow down, girl, or you'll go over the cliff like your Uncle Jimmy, who was simply out gaily collecting gulls' eggs for breakfast when he met his match.

Granddad, say, what effect had he on me, who I am now? I can see him still, sitting slumped on that last bollard before the foot of the pier, eyes staring blankly out to sea, him telling me in that deep gravelly voice that our beloved little island's all but dead. And not so long ago, at least as the crow flies. Just thirty years back, me all of eighteen and an innocent happily married expectant mum. "Why, Granddad?" I asked, putting my arm over his shoulders. And he answered frankly, faintly, as if from inside one of those seal-den caves below "our" cliffs, "I've just seen bottles of milk come in, girl. Bottles of milk in to Cape. Now we're no different from the mainland. We've lost our independence, our self-reliance, and we're losing our very way of life. Come spring, I bet you don't be no more belting feather ticks with barrel staves." He winked.

Near the end, his clothing looked as though it had been thrown on him with a hayfork, or what he called a pike. A bottle of pasturised milk could depress him. But no wonder, part of me says. The 1970s, they were a time of drastic change, and not just in his physique, but in his switch from scything hay and building reeks to puttering. It was as if in three spaces of time we crashed into the twentieth century – not to mention the twenty-first – whole hog. Got free installation of electricity, or at least those of us did who didn't think it a work of the devil. Got running water island wide. Loos and sinks – and the shrubbery near the pubs lost its stink. Bought used tractors and widened our lanes, turned 'em into thoroughfares, and tarred 'em. Bought second-hand Volkswagen beetles. Gone donkeys and drags. Gone ponies and ploughs. Gone one- and two-room thatched stone houses with earthen, straw-covered floors, houses packed like hogsheads with salted pilchard, ten to twenty souls to a household. Gone the family sow. Gone the family boat. Gone the button-button-who's-got-the-button battery-powered wireless. Here imported ham, the state (read EU) subsidised ferry, the TV. Gone the stories in front of the fire. Here the soaps. Gone the dancing at the crossroads. Here tourists looking for B&Bs. Got and gone. Got and gone. I could go on and on.

Granddad died in '85. Grandmother died two years before him – and twice a week for those last years he'd meticulously weed her grave, no matter wind or rain, cold or fog.

Now I'm the one's got to learn to make adjustments, maintain appropriate boundaries, physical, cultural, moral, take care of the gardens, inner and outer.

I mean, weeds, serious weeds: I'm in trouble with my neighbour, if I must confess. And I no longer confess to the priest. In fact, there isn't a resident priest here any more, not enough to go around. This neighbour, I've enough of him, his egotism, his rationalisations, his cruelty. He's like a bullying country. And I've enough of having enough, too. He cares feck all about farming, only about how to finagle grants, subsidies, headage. Days, he studies the bureaucratic ins and outs of the fine print issuing from the Department of Agriculture, nights he scribbles letters as Gaeilge to the requisite ministers and

Teagasc, homing in on the intricacies of government hand-outs. He's discovered that considerably more money's issued to organic farmers than to the little likes of me and mine.

I confess I wince at the thought of Brendan M. classified as organic. He just knows how to be organic on unrecycled paper. He's as green as the grunge on the half-acre of black plastic that covers his heaps of ragwort-rich silage.

Me, I don't have the time to take courses to qualify for grants, what with one teenager left in the nest, six goats, a saddleback sow (the only pig on the island, Mildred is), the milking of seven cows, the garden, and my ritual book a week. Johnny, he does the 70 dry cattle, the barley and oats, the planting and fertilising, the spraying and ploughing, the walls and the lobsters. But the neighbour, oh, this Brendan, he just lets the cattle go, journeys out to the mainland for a 3-day REPS programme, comes back qualified. Thank you very much. Easy as puddin' pie. Qualified. A certificate in organic bullshit. Next year his farm'll be yellow in August, a contagious crop of ragwort. I've seen the rosettes. And on our farm too, our main infestation near mutual dry-stone walls. Boundaries. Boundaries be good for bounding over.

Why, in the last year B's lost 17 cattle out of sixty-seven. Talk to him of timing the shift to aftergrass, of developing a field rotation plan, of erecting mains electric fencing along the cliffs, of pulling ragwort, old buachalán buide, and he stares as though I'm from Mars. Oops, I mean Venus – even if he doesn't know the difference. And not just because I'm a female farmer. He simply won't – or can't – adjust his ways. And I don't seem able to adjust to him and his bully tactics.

Last week, to move a little closer to the point – and his farm's got plenty of them – Brendan's pedigreed Friesian bull, Ciarán, went missing, last seen moseying about his Cape Clear kingdom with the rest of the herd in tow that wintry Thursday afternoon. By Friday morning Brendan has to admit the king has vanished. Late that afternoon he again scours pastures, bogland, peers over cliffs, gives his pride and joy up as a goner. Ciarán's slipped over the edge, been washed out to sea. An accidental abdication.

But on the Sunday, so the story goes – and around here stories go fast and far – Johnny Pat glances across his acreage, which borders Brendan's on the far side, and he by chance looks on over to an inlet, a little Cuas – Granddad would know its name – and from his angle spots a whitish stone where he'd never noticed one before, and the stone moves. Johnny Pat fetches his binoculars and sure enough, there's Ciarán, haunches hollow, balancing precariously on a ledge 35 feet down a vertical cliff face with another ten-foot drop to high water. Johnny Pat telephones Brendan, provides details.

Brendan drives to Mass, waits in the vestibule for me to emerge – he knows I hurt for any animal in difficulty. I listen. I hem and I haw. I see through him. I'm not doing his dirty work again. I dither and I blather. He's all but down on bended knee.

"Are we neighbours?" he asks.

"That's not the point."

"Am I connected to our fellow islanders the way you are?"

"Well." I drag out the syllable and look away, away across Roaring Water Bay, see clouds nestled around its long dimpled peak.

"There. You see. Please."

I decide here's maybe my chance to turn the other cheek, put in motion a plan to stop despising him and his ways. No, I'm not that good. To heck with Brendan: That bloody bull needs saving. In another way, maybe this'll open a healthy gate between our farms.

I contact various Islanders, including my farmer-fisherman husband, my brother, and Pasty the publican. In an hour-and-a-half I've patched together a rescue team, which includes a skipper from Baltimore, who agrees to deliver the digger driver within an hour since our ferry wouldn't depart the mainland until after dark. And I suspect, if I didn't live here on Cape, I'd make one well-underpaid efficiency manager for some low-tech mainland firm. Nervous breakdown, here I come. Imagine working for a mainland Brendan. Betsy, naughty naughty.

When the driver arrives, my Johnny and my once big brother Séamus are in the vanguard to the cliff edge, their tractor boxes carrying inch-and-a-half-thick ropes, slings, the thick nets by which cars are hoisted on and off the ferry. Next comes the digger, cautiously halting three yards from the edge. Johnny, Séamus and Paddy Sean of the Glebe, promptly lower themselves down one of the ropes until level with his nibs, the once and maybe future king.

I'm scared. I mean, Mother of God what have I helped put into motion. The risks. I'd known but hadn't known. I can't not open my eyes, but turn away when Johnny-boy steps onto the ledge into the presence of Ciarán.

Husband and brother begin draping bull with net and straps.

Two men I love and a wounded bull on a narrow ledge above the sea. A simple swing of hips, or head, and some poor soul'll go galley-west into wintry depths.

Paddy Sean, positioned above the critical ledge and clinging to the cliff, keeps the ropes sorted, assists with lowering supplementary food nuggets to restore the bull and distract his attention from the activity around him.

Drawn to the edge myself, I watch the digger's silhouetted bucket, watch mesmerised as its extending and retracting arm operates as if from another sphere.

Dusk falling fast, Ciarán trussed, Steve leaps into the digger bucket and, suspended out over the cliff, some 50 feet up, adjusts straps.

I feel as though I'm on the edge of a different world. Remember the summer I turned sixteen being confined to my bed for two hours every afternoon because of a bad heart and, instead of napping, reading half a book a day, every foxed classic I could get my hands on in the school library, and seeing all around the western world from my little Cape Clear coign of vantage above Roaring Water Bay. Such a change, going through cultural, or psychological, frontiers and meeting Homer and Socrates, Sophocles and Euripides, Shakespeare and Ben Jonson. My chums thought – think – me weird. But I can't help it. Reading's become as necessary as a sense of community. In fact a good book helps to create a sense of another community, one on this little island of an earth. So about a book a week ever since that heart flutter, no matter family down with the flu, no matter hurricane winds ripping off slates, no matter the electrics down and out. I know how to pump a tilly lamp as good as Granddad. And right now I recall studying Greek tragedy in preparation for my Leaving Cert and especially remember the gesticulating master harping on Deus ex machina. And here he is. At the critical moment. In a bucket. Saving my hubby, my big brother. Dionysus at work. Through the boundaries of reality. No, of what we take for reality.

Ciarán levitates. I'm standing, spellbound, mouth open, hands out in front of me, palms up, fingers splayed. The bull's head and burly neck snag under an outcropping. The lads lower him two feet. Ropes and net slip toward forelegs. He dangles, looks as though he's being strangled.

A hodgepodge of us, farmers, housewives, fishermen, lean over the uncertain edge. Two teenage lads dart from beside the digger to a cliff face on the far side of the inlet. Even Brendan has made his way to the scene, staying well back, determined, I suspect, not to get caught up in the drama. He surveys the action. I bet he's taking mental note of who's working.

What if someone dies? I'm partly to blame.

My childhood bedtime prayer rises up unbidden: "Now I lay me down to sleep. I pray the Lord my soul to keep." My beseeching hands fuse, heels of palms press hard against stomach. And I have to admit, however ridiculous it may seem, that I'm frightened not only for my loved ones but for the bull, for all concerned, for Brendan. Brendan, ha! Look at him standing back there, a gentleman farmer, a landlord. Him and his Big House. Me and my fantasies. They know no end. Deus ex machina my foot.

Focusing on a single rope depending from the bucket down to the Greek stage, I realise a slipped knot in it could have consequence, could – "No," I mutter aloud to no-one. Emphatic. Yet pleading.

Ciarán straightens out, gains horizontal balance. The cliff against which he slides up becomes grassy. Someone, Julia, whispers, "Hey girl, here's what it was like centuries back, our ancestors tugging up survivors from a wreck breaking into matchwood against these very cliffs." Millennia back.

With Steve as high in the sky as the bucket can safely go, the boom and stick fully extended, he shouts, "Take in the slack. No, the tractor ropes, you bollocks." Actor or stagehand? or both?

I cringe as he's again lowered, boom and stick swinging through the ever darker sky. "Deus ex machina Jesus, Mary and Joseph," I pray.

The crowd, the audience, we all strain to watch Steve and the bull. We shudder as a group as Steve stands up from his crouch, takes in slack while climbing around the outside of the arm. "All clear!" he yells from his precarious perch.

The digger returns to raising the bull, me to my attempts at prayer.

Inch by inch Ciarán rises. At times he looks unconscious. Or dead. But then an eye flickers, a leg twitches. Once he snatches a tuft of grass. His bulk slides over the edge. He lies limp on his right side. We all huddle around. A tremor passes through his body. Through mine. The men circumspectly loosen the truss. Johnny ties a length of rope through his nose ring and, with a bowline, secures the other end to the rear of his tractor. Séamus pushes both fists into flank, lets loose, leans all his might into ribcage, releases, and I suss out that he's trying to administer artificial respiration on a Greek god.

I stand by the hindquarters, accidentally step on limp tail.

Fifteen minutes later, the last of daylight gone, Ciarán shudders. Séamus jumps away. My old young god in Ciarán guise surges awake, pulls his legs under him, stands, takes a few directionless tottering steps. Everyone scatters, me behind another tractor. Ciarán limps, something wrong with his right foreleg. But he's up, laps fresh water from a bucket, and in the sudden glare of a tractor headlight vomits a yellowy paste of nuts.

Johnny pulls the slack in the rope out, tests whether the bull will come toward him as he increases tension. Ciarán, for once, obeys. Johnny unties the bowline. A dozen loops of rope dangle from his hand.

With tractor headlights behind us, and a gang on either side of him, I help Johnny lead the stumbling bull the quarter-mile to an outbuilding where he hunkers down, can stay warm through the night. And then, noting how bushed people look, I discreetly ask Brendan if he'd invite everyone in for tea.

"An opportunity. The least you could do after what they've done," I whisper.

"The least?"

"The least." How could I have let that out? I'm rude as a fart beside a coffin. "A gesture of thanks," I stutter.

"They enjoyed it. A social experience. And I'm paying the digger driver overtime by the hour, a small fortune."

"They risked their lives."

"They didn't have to."

"They're neighbours, aren't they?"

"You ask 'em in, Betsy. I'll tell herself to shake a leg."

As soon as he disappears, I issue the invitation. The men look at each other in the light of torches. A few shrug. I persist. "Come on, Steve, give 'im a chance to show his thanks."

"I didn't do it for him but for the bull."

"Come on. This once."

"If it'd been him down there, I'd of let 'im rot."

"Steve, please."

"For you, not for him."

I herd them through the back door. Most have never been inside this house before.

In the parlour some flop in chairs as if they've been up all night. While issuing mugs, I notice my Johnny grinning into space. Across my mind come the words, "The king must not die."

And then begins the conversation I've been dreading as much as an accident on the cliffs.

"Why'd he go over in the first place?" one of the teenagers asks in a voice that hasn't yet changed, a voice that rises above the general conversation the way a flute soars over an orchestra. The room falls silent.

"Well now, Éamon," says Iggy, at eighty the oldest present, "if you didn't get enough to eat at home, wouldn't you visit Mikey's house next door?"

But before Éamon can answer, Brendan cuts in. "What do you mean by that, neighbour?"

"Easy, " says Johnny, taking Brendan's arm.

But Brendan shakes off the hand, walks over to where the old man sits. "You saying I don't feed my cattle?"

Iggy looks toward the range, replies carefully, "What I saw over yonder was short grass trampled on the cliff edge, and cow pats as close to the verge as my elbow to my hand. All outside the ditch."

"And what I saw was a man old enough to mind his own business," snaps Brendan. "And not jump to false conclusions."

"You call bones sticking out of cattle false conclusions?" asks Paddy Sean, standing.

"Lads, I'm thankful for your having rescued Ciarán. But that don't entitle you –"

"Stop, stop all this," I cry, coming between Paddy Sean and Brendan. "Ciarán's safe, we're all safe, neighbours, we're–"

"Don't be after interrupting me, young lady," growls Brendan. "Now" – he stands in the middle of the room, surveys his guests – "may I ask you to leave?"

Rising, Séamus says, "Could you tell us, please, so there aren't the usual rumours flying, how many cattle ya lost in November?"

"Four. Four out of fifty-four. And," Brendan adds, as if to preclude further questions, "not from malnourishment but from some inorganic poison. Could've happened to your herd too."

"Poison, is it?" I couldn't contain myself. "You with ragwort rampant? You making silage with ragwort in it? You call that 'some inorganic poison'? Why won't you wake up to the fact that seven pounds ingested kills the liver of a cow? You should be ashamed to be a farmer." I can't control myself. I'm a red-hot wire shorting out. And all too glad to send sparks flying.

"Out, you bunch of begrudgers, get out," shouts Brendan, gesturing towards the door.

Straight-back chairs scrape against flags. Curses sail. I stamp my foot. Noisy neighbours depart into night. When I reach the road, I blurt out to Johnny, "He knows no shame, no shame."

"He'll know my effin' fist–"

"No, that's not what I mean. I mean, if he knows no shame, or if I know no shame, or you know no shame, why–"

"I'll murder the–"

"Then we do wrong." I feel as if I'm in the bucket balancing over nowhere. If I slip, I'm done for. Out of the darkness around us I catch a pulse of the Fastnet Lighthouse beam and I say, "One way we learn right from wrong's by knowing shame, experiencing shame."

We stand there motionless beside the tractor.

"I'll murder 'im if he ever uses you again."

"He can't not, Johnny. The poor poor man." Again the Fastnet blinks, and as its swath of light swings over the landscape way east I add, "Without a sense of shame, we've nothing, he's nothing. I know it's not for me to say and I'm saying it."

"And you can say it again. He's nothing, sweetheart, worse than nothing. Shame be hung. He's no different to a bull without a pizzle."

"Maybe shame helps one step into another's shoes. Where empathy begins."

"Empathy, hempathy. You and your words," he snaps. "He needs a rope around his neck. And remember, little woman, you can't hang a man with a hawser."

We climb onto Johnny's tractor. Tears starting to stream, tears without catharsis, I perch, as habit has it, on the top of the flat wheel well, grip the back of Johnny's springy seat, wonder where Johnny's sharpness toward me and my words is coming from. Despite the darkness and the narrow road, he takes off in third gear. For some reason I'm feeling sidelined, me and my words, me and my tears, and it comes to me like the pulse of the Fastnet through a sea of darkness that I've never even tried to drive a tractor.

The following day I answer the telephone. It's Brendan M., out on the mainland. The vet, he says, reports that Ciarán's in fine fettle, all considered. "Why," B adds, "a month-long holiday with harem in tow on some lowland island isn't necessary, but is highly recommended. Goodbye. And thanks for all your help, neighbour."

He makes a joke. To me. The previous night hasn't happened.

Clueless as to how to deal with this man, I step outside, look across Roaring Water Bay. There's next to no swell. No wonder Johnny said he was going fishing. Not just because of last night. As I take a big relaxing breath, I spot his tractor behind the shed, walk over to it, walk around it, study it, tentatively climb up, settle myself in the seat for my first time ever. Next I know I'm pushing in the clutch, experimenting with the gears, feeling how they slip into place. Here's low low. Here's first. I decide to start with them. I turn the key. The tractor roars into life. I let out the clutch and she powers forward at a crawl. I pull down the rusty throttle on the steering wheel and she goes just that bit faster, louder, but still slow as a snail. Such power. A snail-paced leviathan. I push in the clutch, hit both brakes at once, shift out of low low and into second gear, let out the clutch. And I'm off.

At my slow speed, I realise I can look at every house I pass, every bordering field, and probably as if from a fresh perspective, but I'm too excited to look. My attention level's at fever pitch, encompassing the gears and levers, the switches and pedals, the road immediately before me. Paddy Sean approaches in his banger with the flapping fertiliser bags as replacements for his rear seat side windows. He swings into a lay-by, and when he sees it's me, jumps out of his car, stands as if at attention, and bows as I drive by. And he's laughing. Two hundred yards further along there's another lay-by, into which I pull and stop, let her idle as I peer about from my throne. The sea looks like glass, but as the lazy swells approach the Bullig, they rear up and up and cascade down before they wash over the rocky point altogether.

Yes, I'm learning something from having watched over the cliff yesterday, from having wept my bouncy way home: If I hate someone outside myself, then I hate someone inside myself, and I've had enough of both. Outside, inside, that's the way boundaries work: they don't so much separate us into peace as propel us into war. Look at that break in the townland wall there. Biddy says Jack's cattle demolished it, and Jack says Biddy's did the deed. Thirty years ago it was.

I start up again, turn right at Dinni's old shop, go past Ciarán Danny Mike's pub, don't even need to touch the brakes as I wind along the Blanan road to the Priest's House and on to the Youth Hostel. Brazen, sitting in a man's seat, I drive out the length of the pier, something I never did in a car, as it's too bumpy, for me and my exhaust systems anyway, and I turn around at the very head of the pier, in front of the breakwater, and stop again, soak in the view of the Old Telegraph House and the Adventure Centre, what Granddad always called the Coast Guard Station. On a day like today – and it's top of the tide right now – it's hard to imagine that waves sometimes shoot over its roof. On a day like today it's hard to imagine any kind of storm, even a Force 12 Brendan with waves breaking over my head.

I start off again, at the foot of the pier shift into first and turn right up the steep Glen Road. No trouble. The steepest section of road on the island. Duck soup. I don't even need to pull the throttle down. By the time I'm opposite the Poet's House I shift back into second and shortly I'm up to the lighthouse. Second gear's great if you're in no hurry, and hurry's a work of the devil. I turn around just below the lighthouse. Reverse is simple. I can turn on a dime, however big that is. I stop, lean forward on the steering wheel, look around me out to the Fastnet and then up to the watchtower just behind me. Here's another troubled area. Court case after court case. A public amenity, this national monument, or a piece of private property?

That book I found in the school library, and then used to read aloud to our kids, *The Once and Future King*, it's coming back. Mr T. H. White, he wrote about boundaries, about belligerent ants who claim their boundaries, and then the pacific geese who don't want any. And all those birds we see on Cape, those puffins, razorbills, guillemots and kittiwakes, they all live peacefully, he says, and preserve their own kinds of community without infighting or war because they have no territories, claim no boundaries. Share that, Betsy girl, with the Israelis and the Palestinians. With the Brendans of Belfast. Whether Brendan pulls his ragwort, or feeds his cattle properly, or builds his fences, or apologises. Or not. And accept the territorial black-backs, girl, and don't you be after driving off the king of fishers, that grey heron to whom our South Harbour clearly belongs. I'm Ahab on the quarter-deck; I'm Penelope unknitting; I'm Stephen Dedalus and Molly Bloom hitherandthithering.

I shift into second, head down toward South Harbour, drive by the school, turn right at the cross. When I eventually reach the slipway at the eastern end, I bet I've waved to thirty people and thirty have waved back. And about half are laughing at me sitting here, or laughing with me. No matter. I'm a queen; I'm a nobody. I'm crossing new boundaries, new borders, new frontiers, breaking unwritten masculine law. I'm hearing Emily herself:

I'm Nobody! Who are you?
Are you – nobody – too?
Then there's a pair of us!
Don't tell! They'd advertise – you know!

How dreary – to be – somebody!
How public – like a frog –
To tell your name – the livelong day –
To an admiring bog!

What a bunch we are. With bogs galore. Deus ex machina atop the cliff has introduced me to more than what bulls and boundaries and Brendans are all about. You've got to love yourself first. That's not a selfish act, girl. That's what I'm doing right now, right here, atop this once-upon-a-time tractor.

I pull into the Telephone Exchange's driveway mouth to let a car pass and let the lighthouse thought pulse through me a few more times. Below's a boulder burial. I'm crying. I'm looking through my tears across to Sherkin Island and along the south coast all the way to Galley Head – and even with the tractor roar I hear and see that you can only love others if you start with yourself. That's the way to establish boundaries, girl; that's the way to achieve a start at an ordnance survey of yourself. Now hum up, girl, dry those eyes, and head for the north coast, the petrol pump, and home.

To Be

Practice manoeuvers over – the jibing, the swish of boom as it rocketed overhead like an enemy shell, the tricky triple reefing of mainsail, the sudden rush of spinnaker as it billowed out before them, all completed to the skipper's satisfaction – Mark perched on the pulpit while the rest of the crew gathered in the cockpit to enjoy a sun-over-the-yardarm sip before berthing in Cowes Harbour. He didn't mean to be anti-social – he enjoyed the occasional drink, even more the stories that accompanied it – but he needed to collect himself after the hectic last two hours.

With one hand on forestay, legs dangling out front, his feet one to three metres above the waves, he watched his breathing slow, began to sense rhythm rather than recklessness. The sound of curling bow wave, the change in speed as *The Gannet* surfed down the front of a lazy swell, the privileged intimacy he felt with the sea, what he sometimes thought of as his Great Green Mother, all came together. And he could sense he was smiling not from ear to ear but from full face down deep into chest. Maybe, he thought, here's my Celtic power point, here's what yoga's all about – or prayer. He wasn't altogether certain that there was – or should be – a difference.

Just three weeks earlier, he recalled, when he'd learned he'd been accepted as a volunteer crew member of *The Gannet*, to assist with all sail changes, and be particularly responsible for the jibs, especially for the hoisting, putting out, and half the trimming of the double-sheeted spinnaker – the big boy, the blooper – he'd reorganised his summer holidays.

As head lifeguard and swimming instructor for July and August at the Rosscarbery Hotel in West Cork, he met formally with his staff of three other university students and gave himself, with his employer's blessing, two weeks off for the early August biennial Fastnet Race. His boss, Robbie Kinsella, a thirty-three-year-old physical education instructor from Kinsale, knew of the race, asked Mark for geographic details one early morning while sitting beside the empty pool. He remembered how he'd quickly briefed Robbie with bare geographic facts: "605 miles long. Starting at Cowes, on the Isle of Wight. Crossing the Western Approaches. Running parallel to our south coast. Going round the Fastnet. Crossing the finish line at the mouth of Plymouth Harbour."

"How many yachts?"

"This year, around three hundred. Some twenty-seven hundred sailors."

"And you're now one of them."

"On the lowest rung."

"Good man. Save a life or two from there!"

With that, his boss had left for the hotel's gym.

Legs dangling in the pool a bit the way they now dangled over the sea, his eyes following closely the splashing antics of three young teenage girls who'd just arrived rather than the curling waves below, Mark remembered how he'd immediately fantasised: Why, if I can carry my weight – and then some, and not no drogue – throughout this race, why, maybe next race I'll find myself a berth on a Class I, maybe even in a Zero, and prove myself aboard a 70-footer, not a mere 31-footer like this Class V *Gannet.*

That night, over dinner, when he shared his long-awaited news and fantasy with his parents and grandfather, a recently retired professor of philosophy at UCC, he hadn't been ready for the response. He could still hear his grandfather saying, "Mark, are you sure you're not mistaking quantity for quality? Remember that book I told you about by Erich Fromm, *To Have or To Be?*"

"About man's estrangement from himself?"

"The very one. Estrangement, don't forget, in an industrialised society."

"Well?"

"Aren't you falling into the modern trap of wanting more of something rather than being fully who you could be?"

"To long to be on a bigger, better yacht I'm being untrue to myself, untrue to being?"

"You might put it that way."

"Give me a break, granddad! What's wrong with wanting more experience?"

"Would you not get as much experience on a little boat like *The Gannet*?"

"I will get it, and then, if all goes well, in two years, for the next Fastnet race I'll be on a bigger boat – and get even more experience."

"More? Will you get to know yourself better, or the experience of the ocean better, if you're on a bigger yacht?"

"Sure."

"In that case, my boy, just think now and then of the title itself, *To Have or To Be*. OK?"

"Shall do. For you, granddad."

"For you, my boy. A Zen koan."

Three weeks later, pulpit perched, feeling as though in the middle of a prayer, even in the middle of someone else's prayer, he admitted he was playing with his grandfather's belief that to be a philosopher, one had to be capable of imagining oneself a character in someone else's dream.

A shout from skipper Ger Cotter, owner of Cork's ship chandlery as well as the yacht, brought him back.

"Mark, wake up call! 'Mackerel scales, furl your sails.' No, seriously, toss out bow fenders. We're berthing in five. Wakey wakey, lad. Lower all sails. Engine going on."

Ronnie, Ger's son and second in command, and with whom Mark shared digs at UCD as well as in the minuscule stern cabin on the port side, joined him at the mast foot as they released the halyards, the yacht already pointing into the northwesterly Force 3. The sound of luffing mainsail and jenny quickly disappeared as the crew lowered and furled the mainsail, finally stuffing the genoa into waiting sack. Mark opened the bow booby hatch and, feet hooked on the base of a starboard stanchion, wormed his trunk belowdecks and stowed the bag from his upside-down position.

The next morning, Saturday, 11 August, after a staggered breakfast, and a solid five hours before the race start, Ger called all hands on deck. Kieran D'Arcy and Owen Prendergast, stockbrokers in their mid-forties, and neighbours of Ger's in Sunday's Well, were in charge of the foredeck and all mainsail changes – and first joined Ger in the cockpit. Next came Jimmy Galvin, insurance agent, jack-of-all-trades sailor, who also delighted in being cook. Last, Ronnie and Mark.

Ger had no special news other than that the weather looked good, winds moderate, Force 3 to 4, and that there were going to be six starts between 1:30 and 2:30 P.M., one every ten minutes, Class 5 entries first. By consensus they decided on two nighttime watches, Ger, Kieran, Owen to handle 11:00 P.M. to 3:00 A.M.; and Ronnie, Jimmy, Mark to take care of 3:00 to 7:00 A.M. The rest they'd play by ear, weather permitting, with Ger and Ronnie to serve as floaters, if need be, when it wasn't their watch.

They upped anchor, motored sail-less and slow out the crowded harbour, their wake barely rocking anyone, then hoisted mainsail and number 1 jib to prowl the north side of the Isle of Wight before entering the crowded starting area.

Lunch over at 1:00 P.M. precisely. Time to jockey for position. Fifty-eight Class V'ers approached the starting line, some hugging it, some trying to position themselves so that they could cross at full speed, Ger growing so worried about a collision, a sideswipe, that he ordered starboard and port fenders out. Wristwatches were coordinated by the starter's horn and flag. The countdown began. Thinking that most Class V would compete to stay upwind of each other, contrarian Ger decided to navigate as far downwind as possible, believing that that way there'd be less chance of accident and more enjoyable space. When The Royal Yacht Squadron fired its first cannon, Ger, at the helm, estimated that they were tenth in crossing the line. And the first two yachts had to turn back to cross the line again, as they'd gone over seconds in advance of the signal.

With a light southerly blowing over the Isle of Wight, Ger also determined to stay as far from the island as possible so that shifts in wind direction effected by the island's topography wouldn't affect them as much as those who sailed close to her shore. They wouldn't have to be constantly adjusting their sheets for the ever-shifting optimum trims.

The strategy worked. By the time the cannon boomed for the sixth and last time, at exactly 2:30 for the fourteen Class 0 entrants, *The Gannet* was amongst the first five yachts of the 303, though well aware that the larger boats, now about 5 miles behind them, would go proportionally faster if the wind increased. "In light winds," Ger called out, "small yachts like ours cruise as fast as those seventy-footers. So, lads, here's to zephyrs!"

Down the Devon and Cornish coasts they went for the first two easy days, though on Sunday evening they had to watch the radar closely, as a fog decreased visibility to five hundred yards – or, as Owen said, "We're in a bag altogether." But they ate well, slept well, kept up a light bantering that seemed to agree with the breeze. Mark spent most of his time on the windward side of the yacht – except during the infrequent tacks.

On Monday morning the sky cleared and a northeasterly filled in after a two-hour calm. They entered the Western Approaches. The breeze, as the 6:25 A.M. BBC shipping bulletin had told them it would, backed to the southwest, increased to a Force 5. The 1:55 P.M. bulletin reported: "south-westerly, Force 4 or 5, increasing 6 or 7 for a time, veering westerly later. Occasional rain or showers."

Mark could feel his excitement intensify as he listened to the broadcast litany. A 7 meant they'd be whipping along, probably best a storm jib, no more big boy. And whip along they did. Now they wore their oilskins, both pants and coats, and the stinging spray regularly reminded him of friendly slaps. For him, often hanging out with a grip on the windward mainstay, their seven knots an hour gave an enjoyable buzz, especially on those rare occasions when he could see the keel below him sluicing through the turquoise sea.

At 5:50 P.M., all gathered round the radio, they heard the relevant bulletin: "Mainly southerly 4 locally 6, increasing 6 locally to gale 8, becoming mainly northwesterly later."

"What say, Ger," called Mark from the bow, with safety harness clipped to jackwire, "shall we put up number 4 now? Be safe?"

"Have it ready. Leave on the reaching jib. All in God's own time, lads. Let's eat supper, you youngsters get some early sleep, and by morning we'll reconnoitre, know where we are. While most the top three classes have now passed us, we're near the top in our league. I wager, lads, we'll round the Fastnet late tomorrow morning. And then, if that northwesterly continues, we'll have a broad reach to the finish line, and you know how well this baby surfs your groundswells. And if we can fly a spinnaker on the homeward leg, we'll be in like Flynn in an English race so!"

At 8:00 the younger three curled into their sleeping bags, dropped off.

Around 10:00 the older watch felt the wind increase dramatically. A tap on the galley barometer revealed a drop from the 'H' in change to the 'R' in storm. Kieran and Owen tied a first reef into the mainsail, doused the reaching jib, replaced it with a number 3. But since even that didn't give them a safe heel, they lowered the mainsail that bit more and tied a second reef.

At 10:32, without warning, the three in the cockpit were rolled to leeward, a wave momentarily submerging the deck and filling the cockpit. The yacht swung forty-five degrees off her close reach before Ger could get back to the helm. The next wave, filled with power but not as high, hit them broadside, dumped the sleepers out of their bunks.

Abruptly awake to a different world from that of two hours before, they donned their foul-weather gear, tugging on suspendered yellow pants, which covered them from insteps to armpits, and, at Mark's suggestion, added new security with solid-grip wellies, life-jackets and safety harnesses – and, splashing through water swirling down the four steps into the galley from the cockpit, up they went to discover their companions drenched, shivering, Owen acting scared. The radio, in preparation for the 10:45 P.M. bulletin, Ger had blaring. They all listened hard as the sturdy quiet voice carefully worded the warning: "Fastnet: southwest severe gale Force 9 increasing 10 imminent."

"Some warning. After the storm's hit. Shite."

"How far from the Rock now," Mark shouted to Ger.

"About seventy miles. We're just crossing the Labadie Bank. Probably why these mad seas're rising. A shelving bottom creates steep waves."

"I've never sailed in a Force 10," said Kieran.

"Nor I," Jimmy chimed in.

"Nor any of us," said Ger, trying to see their faces in the dark. "Not something to sail in but to get out of. My father often quoted the rhyme, 'Force 10 is to Force 8 what heart attack is to tummy ache'. A 10's twenty knots faster than an 8 – and the waves grow to twice the height, the suckers 30 to 40 feet high. Could be here already, given what's hit us in the last fifteen minutes. The real danger's not in their height but their shape."

"With such severe slamming, shouldn't we lower sail, motor to Crosshaven?" asked Owen.

"Give up?" said Mark.

"Maybe save our lives," Owen added. "Ger, what do you think?"

"The anemometer reads thirty-five mph," cautioned Jimmy.

"To your stations – which means right around here for now. Safety harnesses clipped to jackwires. Safety before victory. Ronnie, insert the washboards in the companionway hatch to prevent the water that floods the cockpit from going below. Hang on. Wall of blackness coming. You youngsters –"

The Gannet almost broached, the cockpit a swimming pool. Ger realised that he had to give his utmost concentration to steering – and not to anything else. He'd never before felt the helm push him about.

Over the next four hours Ger frequently had to brace his body against the helm. With right hand at three o'clock, he could usually wrench the wheel clockwise to keep *The Gannet* from rounding up when waves struck amidships and she heeled severely. Then when the waves slid under her transom and they surfed off course, he'd battle to turn the wheel counterclockwise to bring her up and keep her from being beam to breaking seas.

A little after 4:00 A.M. the illuminated anemometer registered a gust of forty-three miles an hour. Five minutes later, of fifty-four. Again the waves seemed to double in size. Ger knew he had to keep up some speed, otherwise *The Gannet* would become a matchstick for waves mountainous – and could be buried.

Suddenly the boat heeled over, the tip of the mast catching in a heavy sea. The water ripped off the weather-vane. "Set triple reef," Ger called to Mark. "You're the tallest. Stand on the boom and pass the free reefing line through the leech cringle. Read me? Over."

"Yes sir," Mark shouted back, as he unhooked harness, slid to leeward along the safety line, and, for balance, grabbed an end of a spare jib sheet. He walked forward with the end along the starboard deck, leaning 35 degrees to port to stay upright and bracing himself against the boom with his left hand. Halfway there he bent down and snapped the harness hook onto a jackwire. Up to his shins in water gushing over the starboard rail, he passed the sheet through a block, tied the end to a cleat at the foot of the mast. Then he lowered the main halyard six feet – mainsail luffing so loudly it was as if packets of firecrackers were exploding – climbed up onto the foot of the boom as Ronnie and Jimmy wrestled the snapping sail down against the power of the wind and secured a ring sewn in its luff under a stainless-steel hook on the boom. Then Mark climbed down, helped Ronnie crank the halyard up taut on the winch. So strenuous the activity, they had to take turns at winching in the reefing line that ran from leech into boom. With the reef tied in and the mainsail's area decreased to a third of its full size, *The Gannet* straightened up.

But not for long. By 5:30 A.M. and first light the waves seriously began to cross each other, coming from the southwest and the northwest. The men hunkered down in the cockpit, safety harnesses attached, all watching the approaching waves. Suddenly Mark felt his stomach rise into his mouth: *The Gannet* literally fell off a wave much the way a lumberjack might lose his footing on a log that rolls out from under him. He remembered reading in a physics class that when waves encounter contrary currents, they increase in size by large factors, wave height often doubling.

Mark peered into the lightening darkness, out of which crumbling black cliffs came at them from one angle, and, at the same time, from another angle, and then there was what he imagined ought to be a no-man's land where the two met, their top edges flaring with spume before avalanching down upon them. He sensed *The Gannet* irregularly rise fifty feet, then sink fifty feet, deep into a gorge into which all cliffs crumbled.

With the troughs deeper than the ship was long, and always the possibility of another yacht in the area, there was sometimes nothing that could be done, as when the rudder came out of the water. Occasionally Ger could trailblaze their way through the mountains by finding a wee valley between them and ducking through it, thus avoiding an avalanche. Or two. But not for long.

Shrieks of wind blasted through the rigging. The bow wave roared. Immediately behind the transom the wake sometimes shot up into the air as if a geyser. A sound like thunder surrounded them.

"Here's comes a monster," screamed Owen. "Hold her on station!"

"No, no worry," Ger shouted back. "I can cope with – Look at that cross-wave! We surf down this mother and another's coming toward us. We could play submarine. Or, heaven help us, pitchpole."

"Pitchpole?" shouted Mark. "No way!"

"End over end, man, stern over stem."

"Hang on!"

Waves broke over *The Gannet* from both sides at once. It was as if the sea had exploded and they were thrown up in the middle of the blast. Everywhere swirling water, foam, pandemonium. The boat emerged up into the air again and all, clinging to wires, stanchions, halyards, were safely aboard. And the clear light of dawn let them see the chaos around them.

"Crosshaven it is, lads. Forestay's snapped. We're jib-less. Mayday. I'm switching on the engine. Race over. Douse mainsail. Bag a couple jibs, throw 'em out to stern as a drogue so that we don't pick up such speeds when surfing. Ronnie, report a mayday into the VHF."

"Wind gauge registering seventy-six mph gust. We're in a hurricane!" shouted Jimmy.

"We don't need an anemometer to tell us that, you eejit!"

"Hang on!" screamed Ger. "From opposite directions."

Up and up they rose, up and up, teetered on edge of a Himalayan crest. As the black cliff started to break, they tipped almost vertical, began to dive down the way a knife goes into water. But a dark green wave coming toward them blocked the way forward so that the boat stayed vertical, went deeper and deeper into the water, bow first. The mast disappeared into the sea. For a moment, with bow to mast submerged, *The Gannet* seemed to have become perilously stuck, stopped half way through her agony of pitch-poling dive. The tons of water pushing against her deck from one direction and against her hull from another warred for her possession. And then it was that another wave came from a third direction and broke, shoving *The Gannet* back to a horizontal position, but heeled over on her starboard side. In all the turmoil, she rolled over, keel into spume-filled air. After several minutes of rising and falling while upside down, two heads bobbing on either side of her, she finished her roll – thanks to her structure, the weight of the keel, the smaller waves.

Tugging hand over hand on his harness wire, Mark pulled himself to the submerged ship, climbed aboard, felt the boat powerless, engine off, mast and sails, sheets and stays, dragging alongside, electronic equipment smashed, cockpit and hold flooded, helm twisted at right angles, deck nothing but a wide plank floating about six inches above the sea, *The Gannet* her own jetsam.

Ever with an eye on the waves, Mark peered about for his colleagues. A splash clued him in to Kieran. While the jackwires were in the water, the wire railing's stanchions all down, the wires remained connected to the boat, and Mark was able to pull in Kieran's wire tether and give him a hand as, gasping, he crawled aboard. Ronnie's head suddenly appeared over the bow and he pulled himself aboard, carefully crawled through swirling water to the stern. A wave washed the length of the boat, the men ready and holding on to various cleated rope handles on the protruding galley roof.

When the wave had passed, Ronnie spotted his father's tether. Together, Ronnie and Mark tugged Ger aboard. His head dangled backwards down his spine, his neck slit almost in two by a wire. The little that remained of his heart's blood quickly coloured the water in the cockpit red. Kieran helped a weeping Ronnie lash his father's body to what was left of the rudderless helm while Mark scoured the area for signs of Owen and Jimmy. He found nothing.

Wave after wave rolled by them, through them, slowly lifting the water-filled boat. It was as if the boat itself had become a drogue, a kind of dead dragging weight in the sea rather than, as before, a toy in some mad young god's bathtub.

A muffled shout brought their attention back to their missing mates. Jimmy pointed into the galley and Mark, agreeing, and seeing that the washboards across the hatch had disappeared, removed his life jacket, tied it onto the bent steering column, dove into the water-filled cabin, saw the legs of Owen or Jimmy slightly treading water, and surfaced to where the man's head was in a small, six-inch pocket of air.

"Jimmy, you're alive," said Mark.

"I think so," Jimmy gasped. "But I don't feel anything. Don't know which end's up anymore."

"I think you'd be safer with Ronnie, Kieran, and me outside in the real air."

"What's that mean?"

"Can you dive, swim over the steps and come up in the cockpit?"

"I don't know."

"Well, look, try it, and I'll swim alongside you until you get to the door, then through with you and I'll follow, and push if necessary. OK?"

"I'm not much of a swimmer. You first. I'll follow. But is it really any safer out there? Here's like a womb."

"Safer? Hm. If we roll again, which I imagine we will, you'll be swamped in here, and maybe this pocket of air won't last. Outside, we're safe as long as we can hold on. I think that's the safer of the two places, Jimmy. But God knows. No guarantees."

"After you."

"First let me help you remove your life jacket. I'll come back for it, don't worry, tie a rope to it, pull it through."

Once again Mark dove, headed through the companionway, surfaced. And watched for Jimmy to follow. When he saw hands flailing about near the door, he dove again, pulled Jimmy through. Spluttering, they surfaced together.

"Hang on here," Mark shouted, and, just in time, they grabbed one of the wooden handholds above the companionway.

When the wave had passed, Jimmy, seeing Ger's dead body and Kieran and Ronnie nearby, asked Mark where Owen was.

"Don't know. No sign of him. Hang on."

Another wave lifted the boat but didn't submerge the men. Except for the risk of hypothermia, they felt safer now than when in the buoyant, air-filled craft.

With a coiled sheet Mark went for Jimmy's lifejacket, returned, pulled it through the companionway from where it floated inside, helped Jimmy struggle into the vest.

And then they heard the distant roar of a helicopter. Mark read his waterproof Casio: 7:22 A.M.

Next they knew a wet-suited man dangled on a wire just above and sometimes beside them. Since it was critical to keep his straps from snagging on anything connected to the boat, he had them launch their life raft, something they hadn't wanted to do earlier because they knew that statistically, unless a ship was clearly sinking, they were safer aboard the yacht than on the raft. Another man could be seen leaning out the open door of the hovering helicopter, instructing the pilot how much to raise or lower the craft to keep the distance from the sea as steady as possible.

Once aboard the inflated raft, however, they had trouble keeping clear of *The Gannet.* The oars were of no use in the 60-knot wind and thirty-foot waves, the sea as confused as colliding whirlpools.

In desperation the pilot tilted his craft in such a way that the downdraft from the blade kept the life raft a sufficient distance from the yacht to effect the rescue. At the same time the Sea King struggled to stay just high enough so that the swirling salt spray off the waves' crests didn't clog its turbines.

In twenty minutes, one man at a time, the four were winched safely aboard the Sea King. In another twenty minutes, shivering, teeth chattering, some appendages blue, all well wrapped in blankets, they landed on Baltimore's North Pier and were immediately removed to Bushes Pub, which had turned its restaurant rooms and upstairs into a make-shift hospital.

A week later, Ger and Owen's coffin-less funerals over, *The Gannet* amongst the five missing yachts, Mark returned to work. He shortly found himself, early morning, sitting with Robbie again beside the empty pool.

"You made it."

"Don't know if I made it, but I'm here. I survived. In addition to Ger and Owen, I heard just this morning that it's now official, fifteen sailors lost their lives."

"If you don't mind my asking," said the impetuous Robbie, "what was it like to be in one of the most vicious summer gales of the century – in the midst of the worst disaster in the hundred year history of ocean-yacht racing?"

"Don't know. I mean, I felt as if the whole world was disintegrating, as if we were the only people alive. Talk about being in an isolation ward."

"Would you rather not talk about it?"

"At least a storm's not contagious. And talking, well, maybe it'll help me get back to living with others. Ronnie cried for two days – and two long nights."

"A close call."

"A father dead."

"I've read it was the largest rescue effort in these waters since the evacuation of Dunkirk."

"Yes. Statistics. 136 sailors rescued. 77 yachts rolled over. A quarter of the fleet capsized. And I am here to tell of it. Robbie, what's it all about? Why me one of the lucky ones?"

"That's the kind of question we luckily can't answer. But I'm glad you made it." Robbie stood, patted Mark on the back, walked away.

Mark stared into the water, wiggled his toes, imagined Ger's head one day washing ashore onto a strand where children were building sandcastles.

That night after dinner, Mark's parents motioning that he stay seated and talk with his grandfather while they did the dishes, his granddad started a new conversation by quoting one of his favourite proverbs, "'The sea drives truth into a man like salt.' I'm so sorry for the sting you must be feeling, Mark."

"I've been thinking, granddad. I wouldn't 've been as close to death in a 70-footer, but I also wouldn't 've had the experience of my life. Literally. And figuratively. And now I know size does matter, but not the way I'd thought before. Thirteen of the Class 0 – those big fellas – made it to the finish line out of 14 entrants. One out of our 58 Class V made it. I guess I've learned what it would've been like to be part of the Spanish Armada. Now I know what it's like to be alive.

"You mean, to be."

"To be, granddad, aye, aye sir, to be. Not as in Hamlet's 'to be or not to be' bit. I can't call those waves and winds slings and arrows, though the fortune for Owen and Ger was outrageous. Yes, I choose to be."

His granddad leaned forward, whispered, "Will you ever race again, now that you've seen death face to face?"

Mark leaned toward his grandfather. "Ronnie's already made the decision to buy a yacht in memory of his father – something I agree with – and he's asked me to be his mate. And I've said yes. He doesn't know what size yet. And granddad, I don't care. To be with a friend, and on the elemental sea, that's enough."

Without speaking, they looked into each other's eyes, slowly nodded their heads.

"And how's Ronnie taking the loss?"

"The next boat's to be named *Gannet II*."

"That's action. 'The great business of life is to be, to do, to do without, and to depart.'"

"Ah, granddad, you're the wind puts life into my sails," said Mark. And he started to sob.

"Good man, Mark. I can tell you're not letting your soul fall out of you. 'Tears shed may be bitter, but not so bitter as tears unshed'."

They stood, hugged a hug Mark felt as a lifeline to being.

Calling

Returning from mid-morning walk out to farm's point, Percy slowly became conscious of conflicting sounds, the island pulse: urgent mooing of distant cattle, signifying some herd in need of shifting to pastures fresh, as grass too short, or calves and mums experiencing first day of weaning, or vet inoculating through the bars of some cramped cattle crush; sporadic roar of banger departing, either his father's or the postman's; steady reassuring wash of sea along harbour foreshore.

He entered family cottage. Sure enough, that banger that'd reverberated down drive before he came over crest of hill had been the postman's, for there, on edge of kitchen table, beside the biddy lamp, lay a pile of letters and advertisements. And on kitchen flags, telltale muddy vestiges. Percy sorted through the post, found the missive he'd been expecting for the last two weeks – and carefully, hesitantly, opened what might prove fate.

With back to only window in room, he read aloud the opening paragraph: "You have been accepted at Trinity College, Dublin, to study medicine, beginning this term. Please notify us of your decision on this matter within ten days of the above date." His first choice.

Bless appendicitis. Four days in hospital three years back had given him glimpse of new world, a world where most went all out to help others. He imagined the Regional, with doctors, nurses and staff, anaesthetists and radiographers, helping build hay stacks on neighbours' farms, meitheal after meitheal. He loved the Irish word for a working party, or a party of people hard at work; hoped it would one day enter the English language. And it was that time of summer when he'd best keep an eye on Johnny's lower field.

He sat on the settle. The nagging questions he'd kept at bay, like keeping hens from coming in back door, suddenly forced their entry, pecked at bare feet. Should he go at all? Did he really want to go? If he were to go, would he ever live on the family farm again? Would he not prefer being farmer or fisherman, or both, on this little island of his birth, building reeks (what the American cousins in Iowa called hay stacks), working with a pike, to being in a city, removing tumours, working with a scalpel? What was Dublin but traffic jam, Stephen's Green but specious blip of breather for those on fast track, the Mater Hospital but a flophouse?

So that his parents, when they returned from mainland mid-afternoon – for they and car were gone, had said they might go to the creamery – would know it OK to read his mail, he placed the letter front and centre on the clevy, pulled on a wool gansey his Granny had knitted him, headed for what she still called the out-office – what his parents called the calf-house, he the shed.

Just inside the door, blade neatly tucked behind a collection of shovel handles, two five-foot crowbars, and an adze, the wooden scythe his grandfather had taught him how to use awaited him. A giant scalpel. The worn whet stone he removed from basin, stuck wooden handle toward the sky in back pocket, grabbed the scythe between blade and right-hand grip, and set out for the sloped pasture – its grade too steep for John Deere – way west, the hanging field the family called it, as it was hard to approximate size given slant. He was determined to try to bring this area, which he personally reckoned an acre even, back to life by cutting all the carcinogenic bracken at height of season three years running. And here it was, the third year, the bracken thinner, shorter, seemingly slower to reach maturity, but still rambunctious, ready to multiply. Next year would tell. Always next year.

When Percy reached foot of the hanging field, he stopped, gazed across the harbour below, checking for basking shark slicing dorsal and swinging caudal, seal heads, anything unusual, then scanned far side of island. Not a farmer in sight, not a movement anywhere except for fluttering laundry behind Mary Paudie's house and the cows and wash he'd been hearing before – plus noise of tractor far side of Sleive Ard: Johnny Fineen, he assumed, or Gerry, or both, hard at it as ever, probably hauling cocks.

Placing left-hand grip of scythe on ground, blade at eye-level, he lay left arm along back of the blade, pressed down, gripped it tight between thumb and forefinger, and started sharpening razor-edge with his right. The bit of rust disappeared in seconds, and rhythmic sound of whet-stone, with lighter pitch on run toward tip, and darker, heavier grinding note on movement back, became his foreground world.

In no time he found himself in rhythm as good as that of any dance, but one in which his partner had more to do with his inner self than any swaying sweetheart from school, even Miriam, whose left breast throbbed as the softest smoothest flesh he had yet touched, and whose mind reached as deep as the well below, with water as pure. She'd already been informed she was in at University College Dublin. As he stepped forward with left leg, knees bending that little bit, and body – but neither head nor from knees down – turning toward the left, he launched away from Miriam into cutting swing, a swing he finished at the very moment when left foot had received all forward-moving weight. And as he stepped forward with right, he returned scythe to starting position. With right foot again on ground, the power of the cutting swing would begin there. Again. And again. And again. Here and there he made allowances for change in slope, a stone, a hump; here and there he failed to finish stroke as scythe stuck in unseen briar and he'd have to start swing over, this time with much more oomph; and every five minutes or so, he'd stop, re-sharpen the blade, the pause in physical activity an integral part of overall rhythm.

As he came to the end of each of his two-hundred-yard swaths, he had to be more than usually circumspect with every swing, otherwise some hidden protuberance from drystone ditch would nick blade. At this juncture he'd insert tip of the blade behind bracken stalk closest to wall, or growing out of wall, and start swing there. Slowly wall came into view. He grinned as he compared himself to an archaeologist excavating an ancient site. What are walls, he thought, if not a critical part of the cultural heritage of Eire; why, your drystone ditches, says Da, they surround 1600 fields on this little island alone; and on the mainland, some are so old they run under peat bogs. Percy enjoyed fantasising on what meitheals had built such walls.

In the middle of field, he suddenly became aware of tractor approaching, its sound blotting out all others; then he heard someone calling. He turned. There, on the drive, Colm, bachelor farmer of neighbouring townland, beckoning. Colm, of shortest temper and longest memory. Colm. Beware.

Laying scythe, along with whet stone, beside stile at foot of the field, he vaulted over, ran down.

"What is it, Colm? Gees, man, are you alright? Your face, it's almost purple."

"No bother, lad," Colm panted. "It's me cattle. Could ye give me a hand? The vet's due in an hour and me effing herd've broken out of the crush. Hop up onto the wheel well and we're off. That's the ticket, lad."

Colm braked one rear wheel, powered forward with the other, front wheels turned sharply. The tractor all but pivoted around, leaving a rut, Percy noticed, in the dirt drive, and they were off.

"The bastards leapt over my gates."

"Is your bull – what's his name – Clancy, is he with them."

"I'll give you a pike, don't worry, and if Clancy comes at you, just jam the end of the handle in the earth and let Clancy take the brunt."

As they descended the three-hundred yard drive, Percy had to grip the wheel well to keep from bouncing off. Colm concentrated on driving as quickly as he could. When they reached tarred but savagely potholed lane, he swung up hill, quickly shifted into third. Three minutes later Colm turned into his drive and halted tractor at barn, beside which Percy saw the cattle crush with three twelve-foot galvanised gates flat in the muck.

They re-set dripping gates, tied them together with bright yellow baling twine, tied poles onto their vertical edges, ran bare electric wire round the small enclosure at six-, seven-, and eight-foot-high intervals.

In half an hour they'd finished preparing the crush. All that remained was to herd eight head of cattle, including Clancy, in. The narrow area had small sturdy four-foot gates at either end, with one side barn, the other side what they'd repaired and heightened, and electric fencing sparking here and there above the lashed-together gates.

"Lad, off you go, bring the buggers here. I'll be ready to close this gate and lock 'em in. See, I've a bucket of supplemental nuts here, and when I shake it, you know, the noise alone should call 'em to me."

"Clancy?" Percy'd heard too many stories to pretend he didn't know the danger.

"Clancy be damned. Just bring 'em in. Here, here's a switch, this bit of hose. Just swat any reluctant rumps and they're in like Flynn. Wallop away."

"And the pike?"

"Inside the shed door. Over there. That's it. Good man. Now off with ya. We're almost done."

Percy'd never examined Clancy up close before. Brown as the soil itself, heavy set, neck as thick as three cows' necks put together. His eyes glowered. In his every step Percy sensed swagger. Cock of the walk. Bully. Like master. He smiled darkly at comparison.

As Percy approached from around the back side, and Colm started rattling the bucket, the cows headed straight into crush. Except Clancy. His front legs seemed to Percy to paw the earth. And then the bull turned, came at him, head swinging, body lunging.

"The pike, the pike," Colm shouted. But Percy dropped the pike – which to him had suddenly become a useless toothpick – and hotfooted it to the closest wall, vaulted over, Clancy like a locomotive behind. The wall, four-foot thick and four-foot high, gave way. Clancy shouldered his bucking slow-motion way straight through. Percy jumped far enough to be clear of downed wall, then leapt onto top of remaining wall to ascertain what Clancy would do next. Clancy came straight at him. This time Percy jumped at the last second, but stayed on top of wall and away from previous break. When the new section started to crumble, Clancy seemed stuck for a moment before he powered through. Percy, still atop wall, ran down to nearest corner of field, leapt into next field, hunkered down so that Clancy couldn't see him as he hightailed it to yet another field.

"The pike, you eejit," he could hear Colm shouting. "The pike."

Approaching barn from far side, Percy got close enough to Colm to call out, "I'm here. I'm safe. Do you want me to drive that bloody bull into the crush with your tractor? And you shut the gate once he's in?"

"I'll drive him with the tractor. You wait here to open the gate once he's headed here and close it once he's in."

"No, Colm. Sorry. I'm not going to be on the ground in any field with Clancy. Ever again. You open and close the gate over there and I'll drive in, then you close the gate and be ready here for him. Look at him! He's snorting, pawing the earth. I'm not certain I'll even be safe on a tractor."

"OK, you drive him here. I'll man the gates."

In five minutes it was done, Clancy in crush with other cattle. Percy stopped tractor beside crush, shut it off, hopped down beside Colm.

"Whew," said Percy, "that was easier than I thought. Now you're all set for the vet."

"And when are you going to rebuild my ditches?" asked Colm, who now stood before Percy and looked at him with the same kind of glower Percy had seen in Clancy.

Feeling predicament closing in, Percy suddenly heard himself say, "When I see Clancy eating nuts out of your hand in the middle of this field, I'll rebuild your walls. Then I'll know he's safe enough to approach with a pike."

Colm's face turned even more purple, his cheeks, his forehead, his ears. His fists tightened. But he said nothing.

"By the way," added Percy, "when was the last time you approached Clancy in an open field, with or without a pike?"

"Out," shouted Colm. "Out."

"You're welcome. For risking my life."

Percy turned, walked lane back to family farm, began to breathe huge relaxing breaths as he mounted drive and continued on to stile at foot of hanging field. Soon he was back into rhythm of scything. Soon he could make out sound of wash of sea beneath mooing of cattle.

By dinner time he'd finished the acre, meandered home, replaced the scythe in out-office, learned by phone his parents were spending the night on the mainland, picked himself a mighty salad, à la Miriam, from the kitchen garden, lettuce, peas, tomatoes, chives, radish, broccoli, into which he added some mackerel he'd caught and smoked earlier in the summer. And at ten o'clock, after several hours read of *The Perfect Storm,* a storm he felt he'd been through that day, he hit the hay, ker-plunk.

Next morning he took breakfast tea outside and became aware, above swaying masts and wheeling gulls, of tractor with buckrake depositing haycocks beside rectangular, stone-bordered foundation. The base had already been spread. A flock of children playfully trampled steady pikefuls laid flat by their elders' exertions.

Over the previous two weeks he'd seen four hayfields mown, then Johnny, day after long day, labouriously hand-turning, tossing, tedding cut grass. Then he'd studded his fields with hundreds of grass cocks, later compressed them into some thirty mother cocks.

Grabbing hat and Miriam's ardently vetted bottle of sunblock, in no time Percy was trampling away with the kids. Bits of hay, bits of banter, he felt, covered them all. At first imperceptibly, the reek rose. Now and then someone checked the stack for straightness. Now and then Percy tumbled a kid into the hay, or they ganged up on him and he pretended.

"That corner's a bit proud," he heard from the sweating artists below.

Tramp, tramp, tramp. Every step he tried to compress hay without jostling stack. Back and forth, back and forth. He was in a different rhythm, the rhythm of a beast of burden trudging monotonously round and round a menial yet essential task.

The stack grew too high for the safety of all but the oldest boys. A wooden ladder materialised against the west gable. The work became more serious, especially with wet, heavy fog menacing its way across four miles of sea from the Fastnet Lighthouse.

Periodically Gerry raked the reek. Percy placed his pike along edge of stack, stepped on it. The barber below, with a long-toothed rake, combed out from the sides loose and protruding hay. The reek, Percy imagined, became the kind of frequent customer barbers love.

As the reek grew, his trampling slowed. Three men piked up to him and he now spread and positioned hay as well as packed it. The two boys descended. Incumbent on him was to make certain the reek had strength. He spread occasional pikefuls across the middle so that fresh hay interlocked with that from the other side.

As the reek started to tower, it also began to jiggle beneath him, feeling more and more like a mountain of slow-motion jelly. He wondered how many miles as beast of burden he'd walked already.

As if on cue a parade of women rounded the corner by the nearby ruin. With heaping trays and baskets stuffed, they proceeded to a level patch where they spread tablecloths. The fog had skinned off north, blanketing Roaringwater Bay.

Thick juicy egg-salad sandwiches oozed between fingers. A kind of salmon spread he imagined Darina Allen would give her eye-teeth for melted between his canines. A cool but burning brown liquid coursed down throats. Uisce beatha. Water of life. In scene reminiscent of his favourite sixteenth century painting by high-horizoned Brueghel the Elder, introduced to him by his Appreciation of Art teacher just two months back, he and his neighbours ate, relaxed, told jokes, stretched out.

Freddy curled asleep beside the reek. Johnny tip-toed over, dumped an armful of hay on Freddy's face. Wild shouts, gesticulations, laughter. Kids scampering about. Percy heard one of the seventy-year-olds exclaim, "This is the way it used to be!" He imagined Breughel chuckling in agreement.

Before he'd time to eat his hunk of fresh apple pie, the rest were back at work, so up he went, pie and all, and stuffed in mouthfuls while forkfuls of hay flew his way.

Tramp. Reposition. Push the corner out. Coming from below he heard bits of conversation: Too low to the southeast. Haircut time. Have we enough hay to finish her off? Is that a drop of rain – or a gull? This cock's too much wet in it. Lay it flat, man, not so much at once.

Gerry pushed a mug of water up to him on the end of a pike.

The shortest of the three men piking up now had it tough. Percy reached his pike down and snagged each of his efforts, pulled them the rest of the way up. The top rose to eleven, twelve feet above the ground. Freddy came up and joined Percy. Two on top, two piking, two hauling cocks from adjacent fields, kids raking fields to collect last wisps, the wet stuff they'd thrown out earlier dry enough to be worked in.

After subjecting the reek to another haircut and a severe beating, Freddy and Percy, using pikes like grappling irons, snared an old fish net, folded in half, piked up to them. Presto, the reek secure, covered tight with bright orange, blue and black twine. They beat three more humps out, climbed down rickety ladder, tied stones and heavy pipe along net edges so that winter gales wouldn't send their creation to the Scilly Isles.

And it was finished, cattle guaranteed hay through winter. They gathered up odds and ends, made for the house, where yet more food, drink and banter were passed as they sprawled in the front yard.

Percy returned home, took his only late afternoon nap of the year. When he woke, he peered out bedroom window. There, across the harbour, she stood, four-square, straight, golden. On channels of bedrock. And he knew – as much as he knew he could know anything – that dealing with essential matters had more meaning to him than it had had before. For his own good, for his own little life, he needed to become a doctor. Too bad a tractor does the work of eight men, cutting you off – cutting Colm off – from neighbours, from Breughel scenes. Why, if you don't start with yourself, not with your Mum or Da, or Miriam, or Colm, or Johnny, he realised, you can't do good for anyone. Only then can there be a chance of meitheal. In operating theatre. In backyard. A few moments with a bull and a pike or two, and a neighbour or two, had taught him that.

He'd write his acceptance of his acceptance before bed.

Click, Click

Blow-in Molly Chisom rose early one foggy morning intent on chronicling the off-to-mart procedure. She sought what she called "the raw real". If Irish photographer John Hinde could snap survivors emerging from rubble after bombing raids on London, she, surely, with her Yankee grit, could photograph Gaeltacht islanders loading cattle onto the mailboat. If the locals would let her. If she didn't invade their privacy. If she didn't become too fussy about what they thought of her, whispered of her. If. The challenge was human relations. And herself. The hardest thing to change, she realised, was not belief but attitude.

Over the last two years she'd made a start as a professional photographer. The Cork Examiner's small circulation West Cork News Supplement, issued on Fridays, regularly published her work, but she had more an editor than an audience: he knew her, played her along, published, on average, two photos of hers a month and gave her credit. But no one else knew her. And why should they, after all? Her photographs didn't have, she knew, a distinctive style; people couldn't see one of her studies and say right away, "Oh, that's a Molly Chisom."

She set off, her two goats tethered out from a drystone wall she was trying to clear of bramble and gorse. On the way to the main pier, she noticed, sure enough, that her neighbours' cattle had been before her: unmistakable brown smudges covered the ruts and ridges of narrow lanes; Rube Goldberg contraptions of shipping pallets and barbed wire blocked gaps to pastures; empty molasses barrels interspersed with rotting lumber barred access to front yards. Here and there frayed blue baling twine wrapped sea-salvaged timber in the shape of x's between stone pillars. On dilapidated galvanised gates she'd never seen shut before she deciphered the words "Keep closed by order."

Local colour in dim light. Glad she had loaded a roll of ASA 400, she shot a series of the jury-rigged gates. She knew better than to publish these in the WCNS: Her neighbours might be embarrassed. And she too believed in clean linen, not dirty laundry. She wasn't a whistle-blower. Yet she wanted truth. So she wouldn't not take the pictures. That was it. That was the solution. Her growing archive helped her be ready for . . . for she knew not what . . . for . . . eventualities: One day a picture, perhaps, in The New York Times, The Boston Globe. Or in a spiffy magazine like ISLANDS. Glitz? Aesthetics? Be careful, little upstate New York Molly, you could blow out as easily as in; after all, John Hinde sold out, made the big bucks. How could he have trapped us in that romantic postcard style? Don't get caught, don't catch.

To her her adopted Irish island was authentic rather than picture postcard, honest rather than backward, "raw real" rather than kitsch. That's what people need to see, to learn to see: Values, yes. Not rock stars and fashions but people going about their daily lives. But she'd best be vigilant. She realised her camera threatened, that she could be experienced as a spy, a voyeur. And she feared that she might fall prey to using people. The moment she treated a human being as an object, even if an aesthetically pleasing one, she committed nothing short of evil. That's how evil begins, that's what evil is: treating people as objects. Hang on to that, she thought. Point of reference.

Within sight of the pier, but out of shouting range, she happened upon a posse of cows moseying home, back to the Glen. They sauntered, they sashayed; they had, she decided, the very air of whimsical freedom about them. Up the hill toward her they came, now and then nipping a tuft of dry grass growing out of a wall. She knelt down to try to make them look as though they were looming into the picture. Click – included the harbour behind them in the shifting fog; click – the ghostly green mailboat at the end of the pier; click – the cattle coming on, almost upon her, the purple bell-tipped foxglove beside the ditch.

Standing, she slipped the encased camera into a pouch fastened tightly around her waist. Then she decided she'd be of assistance by herding the cattle back to the boat. They had, after all, already stopped their uphill procession when she rose. But they wouldn't turn when she stepped toward them; they were resistant, downright stubborn, pawing at the earth. Before she could drive them down hill, they broke over a feeble stone wall rather than reverse direction. They traipsed about in an unmown field. It was early July. The tips of the grasses swayed heavy with seed. She had, she realised, unwittingly complicated the situation. "Damn, damn, damn-all," she muttered. "Murphy's Law, you're alive and well on Cape Clear Island and in the hands and wits of Molly Chisom!"

Undeterred, she clambered over the new gap, careful not to twist her ankle in the clutter of stone. She scooted around the cattle – they now skittery – and succeeded in driving them out through the new gap, but, again, they headed homeward. She remembered her neighbour Fineen saying, "A cow, she do nothing but mischief. She do, she do, she do."

Seeing wild gesticulations from the pier, which she interpreted to mean, "Stop them at all costs!", she breathlessly managed to scurry past the cattle on their right where the lane widened into a lay-by. She pivoted, positioned herself – she thought with false bravery – in the middle of the road. She spread her arms and yelled, "Whoa, girls, back you go, old bony 'craytures'. Back, I say! Turn! Turn, you villains!"

They broke by her in a stampede. Fifty yards further on they slowed to a brisk trot and continued along the road to the Glen. With the disused harbour on one side, and enshrouded, craggy, gorse-growing cliffs dropping down to the road on the other, she couldn't get in front of them for a good quarter of a mile. And by then she'd have missed what she came to photograph, the loading on board of cattle. She headed for the harbour.

Wet with dew and sweat from scrambling though the high grass, sneakers soggy, camera tight at her waist, she wondered what guilt she bore, when Matt came ambling up the hill and met her at the top. He explained to her that those cattle had been "sucker bait", meek trained old dears he'd placed at the head of his herd as he drove all eleven down to the harbour. The sucker bait he'd then intentionally turned loose, knowing they would find their way home, while the ones he wanted to sell were penned behind makeshift gates at the end of the pier. He patted her consolingly on the back. Molly couldn't quite tell if he was patronising as well as nice.

When she and Matt arrived at the foot of the pier, a group of four farmers in front of them were vainly – click – trying to coerce three heifers toward the mailboat berth, but no go: one brown maverick broke away – click – and dashed off, frisky and carefree as a rambunctious young bull. Matt and Molly together tried to block her path, but she swept by them with the disdain of a locomotive. Molly attempted a shot of the disappearing critter, but knew it was wasted without proper foreground, contrast. If only I could get one good one, just one, out of every roll, she thought, I'd be happy, happy as a harbour clam. Happy as a Baltimore Bay oyster with a pearl.

Matt leaned toward Molly and said, "Did you hear what I heard?"

"What was that?"

"I could have sworn I heard her nibs say, 'See you next Wednesday, chump!'"

They laughed. No, he had not been patronising, she knew now.

Molly looked for a vantage point from which to view the scene. Partly for her own safety, and partly for that of her F-3, she selected the pile of grey booms by which the safe harbour was closed off in severe storm. She hoisted herself up onto their top, some four feet high. From there she had a firm platform and could command the length of the pier as well as down into the mailboat's open stern deck, where the cattle would – if all went well – soon be snugly tied for the crossing.

She counted twenty-two cattle, seven goats. They were cordoned off at the end of the pier. Farmers and the ferryboat crew, some holding the makeshift gates, constituted a movable pen. The sling was made ready, the boat's hydraulic lift put in motion, and one sturdy beast found herself miraculously flying. Click, click, click. Once the heifer was deposited on deck – click – and secured by halter and rope to one of the ship's bollards, a group of four was herded – click – toward the shipside's open door. Although the tide was coming in, there was still a decent drop, and the cattle balked.

Molly saw sixteen legs brace. Click. One bullock had four men working him over. Ger pulled the halter, George yanked the tail, Fineen walloped him with a piece of plastic hose, Seán pushed against the rump. Click click click click. She hoped she would capture the sense of manure and curses flying, of men struggling all out. His knees buckled as he went in, click, but he righted himself, click. As the men turned for the next, click, the stubborn bullock bolted and sprang out, click, amongst grand swearing in Irish and English. Click.

Molly heard Seán say, "No fear, no fear. Once he's been in, lads, he'll in again. Next time's easy, duck soup. A little tap and a yank on the tail do the job. No hiccoughs, lads!"

The scene repeated itself. Molly tried to witness the comedy and strangeness and danger of the struggle. Cattle bolting, cattle balking, four feet locked against all movement. Cattle and men slipping on streams of dung. Seán would go first for a tail and twist it into a tight circle over the vent. That formed the swirl on which he set his shoulder.

Men grunting, grimacing, panting. The red of hydraulic hoist, the blues of stained boilersuits, the browns and whites and blacks of cattle. The enclosing, intensifying fog.

As if on cue, the sun came out. Molly upped the F-stop, finished off her second role of thirty-six, loaded an ASA 200. She too was sweating. Hadn't Ger tried to turn his face away from her lens even while in the thick? Was she perceived as just a blow-in busybody, or as a photographic journalist, or as an historian? It wasn't fair, no, no, she recognised, to hope the latter. She remembered reading some work by Laurens van der Post in which he remarked that primitive people believe a camera steals the souls of those it photographs. Hey, hey, girl, do you think Capers primitive? Are you guilty of unwitting condescension. That's an attitude to work on, girl.

Are you aiming some insidious, dehumanising high-tech gun at those you like and admire? "No, Molly my girl," she said clearly to herself, "something too much of this. Get on with it."

Since she had the lay of the land, she ventured out to the end of the pier and tried a new angle. Even more light facing south. Aperture up to 18. She made adjustments. She alternated lenses, her zoom for close-ups, her fisheye for bulky scenes, her portrait lens now and then when she could sidle close enough. But best the zoom. It enabled her to be less obvious. It gave her freedom. Maybe. Everything had to be so tentatively qualified.

And then she heard commotion at the foot of the pier. Niall was leading his bull, the one she had heard had gone through a three-foot thick, five-foot high stone wall last week. He couldn't be trusted any longer. He'd pulled out his tether twice. Besides, the calves he fathered often died at birth, too large to be winched out without being crushed in the pelvic passage.

The bull could still, usually, be led by the nose-ring. Carefully Niall walked beside him speaking comforting, soft words, sometimes crooning. Everyone moved respectfully aside.

In the silence Molly could hear Conor muttering over and over again, "Fair dues to ye, boy."

The bull could not make the jump down: he might break a leg with all that weight going with him, or he might so rebel he'd bolt. "A loose cannon like that on deck, dive for the bilge." Matt had come up behind her.

The captain, who oversaw everything from behind the wheelhouse where he worked the hoist's controls, motioned Molly and Matt to get well out of the way. She squatted behind a bollard at the pier's end, ready to jump into the sea, Nikon or no Nikon. Matt hunkered down beside her.

Slowly, the mates positioned the two slings under his belly and placed their ends together in the crane's hook. Click. Despite the muck, the sailors looked as though they were walking on eggshells. Molly captured the look of relief on Johnny's face as the hook's safety flap came down, locking all four sling ends in. The mates stepped back. The captain edged the lever forward. The cinch tightened. Click. The surprised bull hung there, two inches off the pavement, pawing the air. Click. The ship tilted to starboard. Sparks flew from where the hooves momently touched the pier. Niall's relief Molly framed. Click.

And then she concentrated on the bull. She felt as if she had some captured god himself before her and caught him high in the air as he was swung out over the stern deck. She caught, too, the ship's white wheelhouse behind the brownish-orange bull, the green harbour water reflecting the pub, a yacht moored in the background, a look of rage on the bull's face. His bellow filled the bowl of the harbour. She had him. She had him again. She had her picture. She had, she imagined, a bellow from out the sky.

Niall scurried onto the stern deck, caught the nose-rope as the bull was lowered. Click. Niall took several turns around a cleat, and as the bull was dropped to within inches of the deck, Niall took in the slack. Click.

She had photographed clock-work. All cattle and goats aboard, scrunched together, secured, ready for the sea leg of their journey to the mart. She became conscious of herself taking a massive breath, letting the air out slowly, completely. Whewwwo.

But to be thorough, she shot the aftermath: farmers walking down the steps to the sea to rinse their hands, a mate efficiently hosing the skid marks and general muck off the pier, groups sitting about relaxedly having a smoke and chat, a few in boilersuits leaning over from the bridge to observe their livestock. Yes, Ger was turning his face away. Was she within her rights, she wondered. No, rights had nothing to do with it. She was nothing but an interloper. She would let him know she'd publish nothing that included him.

When the tourists going out began to arrive near nine o'clock, the freshly washed pier glistened in the sun, the cattle sent up their odour from the stern. Between the cattle and the passengers metal gates had been tightly lashed together. When they saw the bull, most of the tourists, despite the sunny morning, entered the saloon of their own accord. The captain motioned to the inquisitive that they, too, because of the bull, would have to travel inside. When they started to object, he just said, "In." They obeyed.

As the mailboat steamed out the harbour for the mainland, George went up to Molly and said, "Please, no photographs of me, not in anything. No way. I'm sorry."

She assured him she would never use any with him in them. She wouldn't, no no no. She couldn't, she realised, use any shots without permission from each soul. Maybe it was good that life was complicated.

On the way back to her cottage, she stopped, leaned on the seawall, and stared blankly out over South Harbour, on out to sea. A Galway hooker was sailing across the mouth of the harbour – but no shot: it was all by itself. It couldn't be related to anything else. Unless. And then, realizing she had no answer to her blow-in photographer's predicament, she felt a surge of assurance, almost as if Matt had put his arm around her. "Not all problems can be solved," she said aloud, not caring a hoot if anyone heard her; "the arrogance of the western world teaches us that all problems can be solved, girl, and it simply ain't so. But you can learn to live with your problems, to become conscious of 'em, focus on 'em, hold 'em in view, suffer 'em. That's the best you can do."

The earth felt unusually solid beneath her, the air tasted fresh, rich. She chewed several mouthfuls, straightened up, traversed the long hill home, answered the goats' bleats with a "Hi ya, fellas!" Tomorrow, she decided, she'd work on oystercatchers in flight. On Friday, Matt had invited her to photograph while he guided the mould board plough behind his pony Paddy. Should she use black and white, she wondered, or colour? Both. Could she treat Matt and Paddy as one? Could she click on that "sheer plod" that "makes plough down sillion shine"? She'd see all in due time, she decided, as she crossed the threshold into her island home.

Worm of the Sea

Percy hadn't a clue where he was going, but going he was. Away. Away from the ordinary. Up to here with one-sentence Emails, with date-dropping historical tomes, with tedding hay with his father in pastures east, with toeing the island line, everybody knowing everybody's every move. And he'd already learned – all nineteen years of him – that for the ordinary to have any value, it had to be something one left now and then and came back to. How'd that poem go Jamesy loved to quote their first year rooming together at UCC: "Life, friends, is boring. You must not say so." Yes, if he said so himself.

"Slán, ma," he called over his shoulder as he opened the half-door.

"Where ye off to, lad?"

"The harbour. Not back in five hours, ring the lifeboat."

"Fishing? Feathering?"

"Kayaking. Uh, canoeing." Already, he realised, he was becoming a linguistic misfit on his home turf. So much for tertiary education.

"Ye've yer vest?"

"Lifejacket, flare, pocket compass with mirror, picnic lunch."

"Slán agat go fóill."

He headed straight to the calf house, collected his double-bladed paddle, set off down the dirt road. Every hundred yards, as if part of a ritual, he'd spy a flowering ragwort, put down paddle and paraphernalia, climb the drystone wall, leap into the bordering fern, and, amid cow pats, carefully straddle the enemy and grip the lowest part of the stem with both hands. Legs bent, he'd slowly pull the plant, careful not to yank, so that before the stem gave the silvery knot of roots would come gradually up and up and into air. He'd hit the base of the bugger against a stone to knock loose the clump of earth, then drop old buachalán buide in the road, to be collected on his way home. His father'd lost three cows to ragwort poisoning before he'd understood its insidious nature. Seven pounds ingested, no liver more.

Five ragwort later, while straddling a wall, Percy wondered whether he'd any thoughts that grew like ragwort, thoughts that bred and encouraged similar thoughts, thoughts that could eventually take over inner landscape, turn all to a flowering yellow that, when harvested with hay, turned all to a deadly crop.

Yes, that kind of thought, repeating itself, like right now, made him realise he needed a change of landscape, outer and inner.

As he swung his left leg over and hopped back onto the road, he became aware of a looming presence. Motionless, just up from where Percy'd clambered down, stood neighbour Colum, fists on hips, eyes glowering, face enpurpling.

"Whatcha doing in my pasture, boy?"

"Pulling ragwort, Colum."

"Who gave ya permission?"

"Didn't know I needed permission to pull a weed."

"No. Who gave you permission to be in my pasture?"

"Why, why," – and here Percy, desperate, had an inspiration – "why, the fella up there." He jerked his index finger toward the sky.

Colum continued to glower.

"Are you tryin' to call me a feckless farmer?" he stuttered angrily.

"Just trying to help."

"You could best help by minding your own business."

"Yes, but the seed, the seed from those ragwort, it blows, and on our farm" – he decided to go whole hog – "the most infested areas are closest to our shared walls."

"Is that so? Now you listen here to me, you with your fancy education. Mind your own bloody business from now on. Clear? And keep off my walls. Prob'bly the likes of you who's been knocking 'em down. Now I see what k-kind of man you're growin' into, let me t-tell ya somethin': I d-don't want to see you on my farm again. Not without permission. Otherwise you're trespassing. Got it?"

"Colum, I've walked all over this island, always have. For years. Without–"

"No matter. And say, is it you cluttering up the road with these plants?"

"Yes."

"I t'ought so."

Colum turned on his heel, spat, strode off.

Percy walked slowly down toward South Harbour. Finally noticing he'd been shaking his head from side to side since the encounter, he blew out a big breath and went straight to the kayak, flipped it over, dumped that bit of water out, and carried it to the top of the stone steps. Donning life vest and tucking his lunch and flare under the bow, he lifted the kayak with one arm, his paddle with the other, and descended the steps. Spring tide out, he lowered the kayak bow first into the sea and launched forth.

In no time he'd entered into a rhythm, short crisp strokes, each with that slight flick at the end. He enjoyed the way his shoulders barely turned, the way he'd stretch the bow-reaching blade that extra bit forward just before he dug it in. But he could still feel Colum's presence.

As he powered into the outer harbour, he scanned the sea's surface for seal's head or shark's fin, turtle carapace or dolphin arc. The swells were old, filled with a mighty sense of laziness. And the wind wasn't. The mouths of the caves beneath the cliffs shimmered toward him, black – he imagined – as the devil's cape. Everywhere he looked, he thought, could be art. Pissarro, where art thou? There, as he rounded the westernmost point, four miles southwest, the Fastnet Lighthouse. Practicality in the middle of nowhere; art in the middle of the sea.

He felt he was flying at the controls of an open-cockpit plane. He banked to port. The clouds way south blanketed the horizon, then leapt into faces and animal shapes: an old man with his beard out before him; a baby on his back, knees in the air, with nappy full; a horned cow lowing at the moon. There the swirl of Colum's ear. And then, three or four miles due south, he spotted a feeding frenzy. Up to this point he hadn't known if he'd circumnavigate the island, or go explore a cave over west he'd never yet prowled. Now he headed south.

In a quarter of an hour he neared the frenzy. On its outskirts he stopped paddling and gawked at the commotion. Gannets were diving, black-backs dotted the surface. Four great shearwaters landed amidst a flock of immature black-backs. Common bottle-nose dolphin rose into the melee. One breached.

Percy simply sat feeling privileged to be before a scene of purest nature, nature at feed, mammals birds and fish together, a potpourri of existence. He could hear the dolphins snorting; observe gannets diving from fifty feet up, their wings closing tight for that final torpedo fall toward fish, a lively plume of spray leaping into the air above where they disappeared. He could see sprat leaping, a shoal of mackerel schooling.

An hour passed. The gannets suddenly resumed their passage west, the black-backs headed toward Cape, the dolphins arced their way southwest. And Percy was alone, his Cape but a turtle hump to the north, stone walls dividing up the carapace, not a house in the God-given sight.

As the sea rose and fell, rose and fell, he became aware of his own chest rising and falling. His hands rested on his paddle, his paddle on the cockpit coaming. Now and then a storm petrel darted past. One headed straight for his paddle blade, took evasive action that split second before collision. Naa naa, he could hear it tease as it ducked into trough after trough and disappeared.

Soaking it in, and devouring his picnic, he knew it wasn't the wisest thing in the world to stay this far out. If a strong wind sprang up out of the north – and there was a cloud bank that direction – he knew he could be blown away, no one the wiser. But he also knew that sometimes you have to be a little bit crazy – or else you go a whole lot crazy. Maybe Colum's outburst had been his little bit. Then wasn't this little foray being that little bit crazy? Wasn't it–

A flicker caught his eye. Fingers tightened around paddle. Elbows perked further out from sides.

Yes, transparent, translucent. Flapping slowly from side to side. A piece of some membranous substance half an inch thick, a foot tall. And now moving, slicing the water. And floppy. An exotic fin. Cautiously, catfully, he paddled toward it. Ten feet off, he braked, held the kayak steady. And there, through green-glowing but pellucid waters, he stared straight at a creature he'd never before seen, its pectoral fins diaphanous. He couldn't stop himself from fantasising he was in on a sighting of an underwater angel, albeit of all but awkward dimensions, but so at ease, relaxed, unafraid – and luminous, numinous. The caudal fin, as it moved in a kind of slow motion, appeared as wide as the fish was long, and it too reflected light. Where he would have expected the dorsal fin to emerge he saw zigzag lines, almost black, that looked like runes, or letters from an ancient Hebrew alphabet. Oh Orthagoriscus mola, he breathed aloud, articulating the Latin identification he'd heard in a marine biology class. Oh mola-mola. Holy mola.

The creature, while not significantly longer than the kayak, communicated to Percy a connection to infinity. And as the presence slowly moved around him, as if vaguely curious about the interloper, Percy could feel his own left-brain labelling, pigeon-holing, western worlding, grind to a halt; could sense his scientific identification of sunfish sink like jettisoned ballast into Davy Jones's maw of a locker.

Beneath and beside him, in a gentle guise, he imagined what his grandfather – and other old greybeards of the island – had referred to as a worm of the sea, what he'd always assumed some maverick shark conjured up into make-believe fireside tales. Over hypnotic swells Grandfather Cuddy's words floated back: "Percy, you never know what might appear out there, what might lash out, a worm of the sea. The very divil incarnate." Devil, he thought, seeing the runes on the slow-motion creature's back. Could angel and devil be interchangeable – depending upon where you sit? Could their very nature be dependent upon perspective? Worm of the sea, devil, angel of the depths, one and the same?

As he watched old mola-mola circle about, words Father Jimmy'd shared with him after Mass one day last year drifted back, "My son, 'tis time to reassess this world. Jesus, He was a reassessor. He tried to help us change from the belief that we should demand a tooth for a tooth and learn instead to turn the other cheek. Tell that to your Unionists and Republicans, to your Zionists and Hamas. And now we, too – we priests of the Church – need to stop telling everybody what to do, what to believe: we've proven ourselves as fallible as anyone else, more fallible. We set ourselves up as your moral directors and became self-appointed dictators when we should have been servants. I fear we've called some angels devils, some devils angels. Caritas should be the judge."

Love, yes, holy moly, Percy thought, watching fins change colour, watching mola-mola roll in the water like some kind of condensed, made-flesh rainbow. He felt something welling out of him, a feeling of love, love for a floppy fish; he felt his soul's skin being marked – even given a touch of shagreen – by a worm of the sea.

Oh, Percy! What nonsense, Percy! What conflicting levels reality's got. Keep this to yourself, boy. All – maybe except Father Jimmy – they'd think me nuts, Colum's case proven.

The sunfish dove, disappeared. While Percy stared after it, he also became aware that the sun itself was nearing the horizon, that it was high time he headed home. He genuflected, laughed at his absurdity, dug in paddle.

King Conger

Johnny, an island man with seven known generations of islanders behind him, decided, late autumn, to go for broke – and extend his boundaries. He'd stored sufficient hay for the cattle and, he joked, sufficient potatoes for his family to see them through another winter, to make his decision.

First he convinced Deirdre, his wife of four years and mother of their three children, that there was more money and less bother in part-time lobstering than in full-time farming. "Blast ragwort," he'd told her, "and all them chemicals necessary to keep weeds in check. All them regulations, forms, winks and nods, to harvest grants. Why, I need to invest in a creative accountant more than in a modern John Deere. And blast the curiosity of cattle – not a one without mischief in 'er. Why blast even Patsy – not to mention her ilk – who requires my help through a half a week of nights just to give birth. This poor arm's had to go in her back door over and over again to fiddle how calf comes out. My dear, Mother Nature's one tough cookie."

Next he'd twisted his Uncle Paddy's arm to let him renovate the *Saint Columba*, not quite tucked into the back shed, the twenty-three foot boat in which he'd played by himself as a boy and even then had imagined riding the high seas, with himself as captain.

And finally he'd persuaded his foxy-friendly Skibbereen bank manager, Danny Donoghue, to loan him £15,000, with which he bought the paint, lumber, oakum, caulking compound, and second-hand replacement engine for the boat, 400 new double-throated pots at a discounted £25 each, a mile and a half of two grades of rope, one for the main lines for the strings of pots and the other for the thinner leads to each individual pot, thus more or less assuring that if a rope were to snap, he'd lose a single pot rather than an entire string of 25.

And, by the next spring, on 23 June 1999, according to his log, with inexperienced fisherman and good neighbour Diarmuid as mate, off he went at first light, three strings of pots – all the boat could hold – piled carefully in the stern, each pot baited the afternoon before with a head or side of rotting mackerel, or a chunk of ripe rabbit, each pot in an order so that they could be tossed one after another off the stern without any snarling complications.

Johnny'd thoughtfully elected to shoot so as not to disturb any fellow lobstermen. Instead of selecting a popular stretch around the island itself, and warring with whoever normally fished it – Ronnie, Ger, Aidan, or even all three – he motored out near the Fastnet Lighthouse. Four miles further out to sea than his Cape, its distance – and its savage reefs, its tidal races, sometimes so loud you could hear them snapping – had long dissuaded the other local lobstermen from hanging out there. But Johnny knew the waters, liked the challenge, and he and Diarmuid together had studied the irregular, deeply channelled bottom not only on nautical charts but also with his own echo sounder. They'd quartered the waters around the Fastnet the way a marsh harrier quarters land. Consequently Johnny was certain they were safe enough, if they shot the pots carefully – and kept a wary weather eye on the horizon. They were sure the region hadn't been over-fished for years. Lastly, Johnny had to admit that for some perhaps superstitious reason, he also felt more relaxed, more safe, out around the Fastnet – no matter that it had been automated ten years earlier – than he did along some of Cape's stretches of jagged shoreline. Especially out from the island cliffs, he'd noticed, the crosscurrents had a way of playing tricks on him, and the swells had a way of crashing into the foot of a stretch of sheer cliff, then full steam reversing direction so that he had to battle movement from conflicting directions.

Three mornings later, the last string – the sixteenth – shot, the final marked buoy designating its end tossed overboard, Johnny signalled to Diarmuid that he was going to pilot the *Columba* back to the first line they'd shot and haul it – start making money. Once there, the two orange buoys marked 1 and 1A clearly visible and a hundred-and-fifty yards apart, Johnny asked Diarmuid to man the wheel.

Diarmuid sidled the *Columba* up to this first of sixteen strings. The tide slack, Johnny snagged the line with the gaff, pulled the buoy aboard, began hauling. As he lifted the first pot off the bottom, he could feel some weight to it, grinned at their luck. But then he began to worry that the weight was too much for a lobster. When the pot came into view, through the pellucid waters he spied a thick ball of shiny blackness. Within lay a conger eel, curled round and round and round, not a good omen, this, the most powerful fish for its size that any fisherman can catch in Irish waters. Even Aristotle – according to well-read Uncle Fineen – claimed this brute "born in the bowels of the earth." The razor teeth. The speed of strike. The power of serpentine body. The trail of slime it leaves on floorboard, side-deck, coaming, rub rail. The memory it sears on mind.

Yes, Johnny'd somehow forgotten all about congers – or even repressed their existence. But on seeing this denizen of inshore sea ravines and harbour lairs, he was dumbstruck, honestly filled with numbing dread. A memory – like his thick yellow non-breathing oilskins – enveloped him.

He – all ten or eleven years of him – was out in a little punt with Uncle Fineen, out near the wide mouth of South Harbour. At the oars, he watched closely as his uncle hauled the last of five pots on his only line, watched him as he hefted this pot aboard. Within lay the only catch of the day, a conger. For mischief's sake, instead of releasing the bottom feeder off from the side of the punt, his uncle opened the pot in the stern and dumped the snapping monster into the bilge. It writhed about, finally stretched out, six feet of ready muscle. To feel safe Johnny, hand to mouth, perched on his narrow thwart – and even then he had his doubts – and his uncle stood on the spacious stern seat. Johnny watched in horror as Uncle Fineen poked the conger with a bamboo pole, tiny prawn net at its end, a present Johnny'd received for Christmas the year before. The conger struck the pole the way, he imagined, a cobra strikes a victim. The pole snapped in two as if a dry twig. Finally his uncle grabbed an anchor and, waiting his chance, hands around the shank as if it were a sledge hammer, smashed the sharp-edged crown down on the conger's head, stunning it before he stuck his fingers in the little pockets behind the conger's head, there, just in front of the tiny pectoral fins. Then his uncle lifted the conger into the air and heaved it, slowly twirling, overboard, crying, "Long live King Conger!" Johnny'd been afraid of congers ever since and, believing them mainly an inshore fish, innocently thought he'd be conger-free out at the Fastnet and hadn't given them another thought. Until now.

Still, Johnny lifted the first pot aboard, stored it in its place, kept hauling. By the time they'd all twenty-five pots piled four high across the stern, the first of the sixteen lines hauled, he shuddered at what lay ahead. Ten of the pots contained conger – around three hundred pounds of eel altogether, he reckoned – two a lobster each, the rest a variety of crab (including one spider), sea urchin, dogfish, starfish, and one a tiny pipe fish, the size of three pencils end to end. But the eels. He knew how caught conger could play dead for hours in the side yard grass – and strike at nightfall. He knew that once dead, spine severed, with their skins cut around their necks, they could be hung by their gills from the eaves, with a couple of bricks tied to the skin, and by morning the dangling predators would have their slimy skins stripped off and be ready for gutting and the pot – if one could stand eating them, which he never could. He knew, too, that if he opened the pots over the gunwale, the conger would slither off, ready for another free meal in another pot another day. He also knew that if he opened each pot aboard, and hit the eel with an anchor, he might miss, or it might get him first.

He gestured to Diarmuid to place the *Columba* in neutral and come take a look.

Diarmuid stood in the wheelhouse doorway, stared at the haul, muttered, "Bollocks."

"What would you do?" Johnny asked.

"Those buggers have eaten our catch. They'll eat us, if you're not careful."

"But what would you do?"

"I'd cut off their heads."

"Have you ever tried to kill a conger."

"I know, they're strong as elephants, and quick as lightning. Best to break their spines."

"If I just let 'em back in the drink–"

"–they'll visit us again. Yeah."

"Yeah, it's us against them. War, man." Johnny paused. "Would you try something, something my uncle once taught me. I'll let one loose here on the–"

"–Not with me here. That wasn't part of no agreement, neighbour."

"Let me finish."

"All yours, boss."

Diarmuid saluted, stepped up into the wheelhouse, turned, watched from the doorway.

Johnny saw that he was, for all intents and purposes, alone. He knew full well that if he didn't do away with the conger, they'd keep coming back, give him no chance for a livelihood out by the Fastnet. He'd have to significantly decrease their population before he'd have lobster, a lobster in a trap nothing but a fast food snack for a conger. Blast and double blast.

He stood there, looking at the tiers of pots, the customs officers, his upper front teeth clenching his lower lip. Four hundred yards west the Fastnet loomed like an impartial but mighty power watching his every move, able to read and test his every thought. He could hear the wash around the base of the Rock. He could hear Danny, the bank manager, knocking on his front door as the bank began the process of claiming his house as collateral. His dream of lobster had become a nightmare of conger.

Johnny had the sensation he was standing on the border of an alien country, a country whose language he didn't understand, a country where one strain of the inhabitants might murder him the moment he crossed over.

Then he could hear Uncle Fineen laughing at him from beyond the grave.

Uncle Fineen. What would he do, Johnny wondered, in this predicament?

As he gestured to Diarmuid to stay in the wheelhouse and watch, Johnny un-cleated a rope running from the top of the short mast to the base, let it out, tied a slipknot near the end; then carried a six-by-six-foot plywood board nestled between the green plastic fish boxes and the front of the wheelhouse to near the stern, slipped the loop of rope around one end of it, positioned the other end of the board against the outside of the starboard coaming, lowered the board until it was flat and jutted out from the boat like a wide rail-less gangplank going nowhere, and cleated the rope afresh.

Johnny had his workspace.

Then, as if he were passing through customs into the murderous alien country, he walked the three steps to the mountain range of pots, lifted the last pot to come in off the top, unclipped its two half-sections, the eel seeming dead, and, with panting trepidation, dumped the glistening coils – the body roughly twelve inches in circumference – out onto the workspace. And like lightning, before the slimy snake could either attack like lightning itself or slither away into the sea, Johnny darted an index finger into each of the pockets beneath and behind the eel's head, lifted the six foot powerhouse into the air, swung it around so that its sinewy long body straightened out behind his back, whipped it up and over his head, slammed the first few inches of King Conger's neck down onto the half-inch wide coaming, hoping his spine would snap. Only then did Johnny yank his fingers out – and away.

To Johnny's relief – and Diarmuid's amazement – the eel slowly writhed off the workspace into the brine and, with spasms and slow-motion twitches, sank from sight.

Johnny felt as if his proffered passport had passed muster and that he was starting to speak a local language new to him, Congerese. Crabese he already commanded.

From behind, Diarmuid clapped, rejoined Johnny.

"That's what your grandfather used to do?"

"Never saw him do it, but, I confess, he once told me the story of how he did it."

"But the risk, Johnny. You miss when you go for those gill-holes, or whatever they are, and, hey boyo, you've lost a finger – or a hand."

"Yeah. I've heard those stories too. Can take your knee off, one bite."

"How 'bout your throat?"

"Anyway, I'd forgotten the stories. But now I understand something I hadn't thought of. It's the start of the lobster season. If we don't discourage these eels, we'll be catching mostly them over and over again. So we cripple 'em like that, and we're in the money."

"You cripple 'em like that, not me. Jesus, Johnny."

"Don't tell nobody. They'd prob'ly sic the RSPCA on us, cruelty to animals. But then, who isn't cruel, tell me that? Why, you can't send a cow to market without being cruel. I prefer a livelihood to a coterie of greedy conger knocking daily at my door demanding brunch."

They laughed. But when Johnny took down the next eel-filled pot, Diamuid again retreated to the wheelhouse.

Within half an hour Johnny had similarly disabled the remaining nine conger – without a mishap. The secret, he concluded, lay first in the mindset, the determination, then in the speed of attack. Now he knew why Uncle Fineen, quoting, or so he said, some French fisherman, occasionally entoned "Doubts are more cruel than the worst of truths."

Within a week Johnny'd broken the backs of one hundred and twenty-three more. Over the next month he caught only ten. By the end of September, with gale season upon them, they moored the *Columba* in the safe harbour for the winter. That night Johnny tallied their total catch, on average one lobster for every five pots hauled, a bit of profit even with the debt paid off. And the crabs paid for Diarmuid.

Decision made. Henceforth, weather willing, Johnny'd be part-time fishermen, part-time farmer. He'd go with the seasons as well as with the weather.

The next day he collected the remaining lobster and crab from his holding tanks outside and west of the mouth to North Harbour, piloted the *Columba* to Baltimore's North Pier, sold the catch to the fish union, then drove his mainland van to Skibb and in person handed the total cash repayment, plus interest, for the loan over to Danny – and presented him with a seven pounder, claws tied shut, at the same time. How the tellers had guffawed to witness a live lobster pulled out of a battered briefcase flap its tail on the counter under the manager's nose.

Home that night for the only lobster dinner of the year, Johnny told Deirdre he suspected that next spring the first Fastnet shooting of pots would quickly put despot King Conger in his place. "After all," he whispered over dessert, "as a consequence of Uncle Fineen's nomination, the Fastnet Lighthouse late last night issued me an honorary passport. Come June I'll be free right off to fish the bottom kingdom to my heart's content."

Deirdre hissed right back, "Don't be after tempting the King."

Belated Rite of Passage

Dedicated to George Underwood, Jr., Arnie Mindell, & Paddy O'Leary

Somewhere between the ages of three and five, Deghlan Delaney had had a dream that periodically flooded him with ricocheting bars of light, even now, at fifty-nine. When the dream surfaced, like a trench-bottom fish breaking water, he felt as though what had happened then was still happening now, or, as he sometimes fantasised, now was then . . . then now, time but a handy construct of the mind, the body, not, no no, of the spirit.

He assumed his myth implicit in his dream, but which myth – bloodsucking leeches of god-almighty analysts – he still wasn't sure. If Greek: Sisyphean labour, dammit and make the best of it, Camus style; if Mesopotamian: Gilgamesh breakthrough in search of life everlasting for his hairy friend. Please, dear gods, he mischievously prayed from what he had come to regard as his precarious perch on the bountiful tree of life, the latter; but if the former, let my downhill walks be rambles full not so much of decadence as of silly wholistic dalliance and middle-aged lyricism, if such beast be.

"Dreams don't give two hoots in hell about the freaking clock," he'd tell his wife, arms flying about in absurd gesture; "your earliest dream, like your earliest memory – if there's any difference – works prophetically, carries your seed, acorn to your oak." For more than the pure fun and pain of it, but for these too, he had participated in dream workshops in the meandering foothills and ravines of the Green Mountains in New Hampshire, gestalt therapy sessions at the Easlin Institute above ocean-hugging Highway 1 in California, neo-Jungian process-oriented hands-on psychological training-weeks in the flower-strewn Alps of Graubunden and beside the agate-pebbled growling strands of Oregon.

Process-Oriented Psychology. POP. Pop goes the weasel. POP goes the pompous ass. Yes, old Pop-Pop, you who clicked your nails together to call me to morning porridge. So POP it is, he decided after a decade of your classical Jungian dream analysis, that's the ticket, the way, no, one way, my way, highway to the whole Self, ta-da, ta-dum! Roll of kettle drum. Sennet of trumpets. Counter-rhythmic thump of bodhran to bring him back down, to puncture his easy inflations. Snarling bagpipe in the ear. Bless all chthonic utterances. Humbaba.

The last seminar he attended was held alongside Lake Geneva, in the modest resort town of Le Bouveret, a mile from the Swiss-French border. The participants may have been freaky, but full of fun, alert, compassionately confrontational. They acted as if they were twenty years old yet had insights of old souls. Myndy, the leader, looked, in some lights, a shrunken Asian, weathered on the peaks of the Himalayas, schooled in the ashrams of Tibet. In other lights he appeared a thin, sinewy Israeli, anywhere between the ages of forty and sixty-five. Or an Eskimo trickster. Or Coyote. His prominent forehead shone. His wrinkles looked more the result of laughter than of suffering, but then again. . . .

Deghlan was not surprised to discover that Myndy's first Ph.D. was from MIT, in physics; his second, from the University of Zürich, in psychology; his first professional diploma, from the Jung Institut, Küsnacht.

"Yikes," he recalled, comfortably standing beside Deghlan, since it was precipitately Deghlan's session, "the event of being labeled a certified psychoanalyst, that threw me. I started seeing patients, clients, analysands – guys like you, guys like these guys" – his gesture included all in the circle closing around them – "and me, and for the first year, I had to take a dump between each session, that's how sure I was inside myself. And then I started to see that the body says as much as dreams, and that when you work with both, well, wow! You get into process, you come up against edges, and edges are where you've the possibility for growth." As he spoke, he danced like a boxer around Deghlan. They squared off.

Myndy feinted a few punches towards Deghlan's face, and then caught him lightly in the solar plexus. The wind came out in a loud "hunnnk". Deghlan regained his balance, his breath, dropped to one knee, and tackled Myndy. Once a high school wrestler, Deghlan turned Myndy over onto his back. The imp in the analyst looked disarmingly up and said tauntingly, "Come on, D.D., tell us the dream, tells us your first dream."

They looked at each other, neither moving. Deghlan slowly lessened his controlling grip.

"Hey, hey," said Myndy, still prone, looking up, "we were boxing, and I had you, and you shifted to wrestling, and you had me, and I've now shifted into work mode – and now you, you nitwit, you've yourself."

Myndy sat up, his arms behind him on the floor, and pulled himself backwards along the matting.

Deghlan looked around. Twelve pairs of eyes waited. The participants scuttled into a semicircle before Deghlan.

"I was in–"

"Tell it as though it's happening now," quietly interrupted Myndy.

"Yeah, you nincompoop," said Trinkie, "you sissified psycho-pomp." Laughter. Her session the previous afternoon had initially revolved around her tendency to let even a bureaucratic letter rile her up. The session had ended with her recognition that evil, insidious creature, occurs whenever one human being, let alone an organisation, treats another as an object. She who didn't like being labeled, being treated by labels, had just consciously labeled him. Her tears remembered, he let go.

He first scowled lightly at the group as if to acknowledge no more than that his ears worked. And then he eyed the group, slowly catching each person. He took a deep breath, set forth:

"I'm in a tunnel, long, long and dark. I feel rather than see a pair of wild hares nipping at my heels, herding me, driving me on. The hares were my lovely, cuddly (OK, guys, everyone's entitled to some romantic diction) furry slippers, but they've metamorphosed into living, hungry, snarling creatures, and turned on me. I'm running, sometimes scurrying, to keep from being devoured in itsy bitsy (there I go again) sinister mouthfuls."

"He's doubly conscious, you guys," whispered the leader, perhaps teasing yet alerting Deghlan; "he's able to be in both worlds at once. Watch his body now, not just his words. Watch for what he repeats in gesture, in diction."

Deghlan now sat cross-legged, Indian fashion, his hands inscribing circles.

"The sides of the tunnel were – oops, I'm interrupting myself, I'm falling out of tense – are, yes are, the sides of the tunnel are damp, cold, constructed long ago of huge stone hunks, granite ashlars. Whenever I stop for breath, the hares soon catch up and start their horrible nipping, a molestation that has, if not death (boom boom!), lingering suffering its goal. (No, it's not melodrama, Trinkie.) Mother hare. And father hare. (Reductio ad ovum, guys.) I want to scream and scream, scream so that my insides pour out, molten, rage as never man raged, but I also want to escape the tunnel – and I sense that if I give in to the 'primal' impulse, I'll never succeed in accomplishing the paramount, for at the end of the tunnel gleams a small circle of golden light, a distinct but vastly distant pinprick of possibility. Sunrise promise. While it doesn't appear to grow larger the longer I run, not to run would be to surrender to the tyranny of the unjust marauding petty, the archetypal cop-out (get that, pals from California)."

"On with it. Don't be so self-conscious, D. D."

Deghlan stood up, slowly started to run in place. Straight lines replaced circles.

"Without sleeping I'm forced to run the entire day, the night, the second day/night, the third day/night, day/night, no diff. I'm aware of my hands pumping at my sides: sometimes they're open, slicing into the black air, and other times they're clenched, fists, and batter my way forward, scared stride by scared stride. On the fourth day I begin to discern a dim light along the length of the tunnel. I don't notice when it begins to appear, I've become so mechanical, a mechanism, life reduced to a monotonous strained motion; yet the continuous running is the only way to survive. I'm the still surviving perfunctory. On the fifth day/night, when I look over my shoulder, I actually see the hounding hares. Their back legs powerful, the hind legs on kangaroos; their oversized, protruding front teeth shine a clean white in the growing light. On the sixth day I feel the air freshening, I notice that the bumps on the rough stones begin to cast slight shadows. On and on. And on the seventh day the light becomes brighter, with each slow stride brighter. Soon it's almost blinding. I don't mind: I can eat the air, drink the fresh wind. I feast as I flee. I feel energy filling me, flowing through me, through my tired limbs, through my tired old ticker."

He enacted a stumble, caught himself. His face became haggard, an El Greco cruci-fiction. He tried to look around the circle of faces. Smiled limply.

"I know, at last, that I can, will, make it. I suddenly realise that the hares have turned back some time ago; I haven't had to shake the buggers off for hours. I slow down. I'm gasping, permitting myself the liberty to gasp. I suck in delicious lungful after lungful. I walk. I walk and walk. I walk out into light. Out, safe, solitary. I don't know where I am, but I'm infinitely relieved to be here. I lay me down, down on hummocky, warm, multifoliate grass. And sleep."

He fell to the floor. The group cheered. They came up to him. They swirled about in a huge embrace, falling on him. A mound of bodies.

That was his dream, how he told it under the Matterhorn during that "first-dream seminar" one wet July. He hated the tunnel, but it was, he knew, his adventure, and he accepted it, welcomed it, wanting it to burst into open air. In its own time.

And this was his memory, albeit an accumulated one, one that grew over the years but which began when he was four and ended when he was twelve, the June of 1950 when both his maternal grandparents died within a week of each other, their house sold within a month, and his grandfather's labyrinthine collections of stamps and maps and valentines auctioned off for peanuts within three months of his funeral. Deghlan wrote the memory in his journal that same seminar, which then, like the other participants' journals, was circulated through the group one afternoon and evening. He wrote:

'In the summers, when able to visit my grandparents, I loved nothing more than to walk down the long cool upstairs hallway, past the door to Gramma's bedroom suite, past the door to my grandfather's little nook, past the guest room, which once had been my mother's bedroom, past the door to the main upstairs bathroom, and then, instead of continuing down the hallway to the top of the back stairs, and all the linen closets, and the maid's room, I'd turn left, into Grampy's study, and there, cross the room slowly and finally sit in the armed wooden swivel chair before the huge desk – and gaze about as though to each object I'd devote years of scrutiny and adoration and pride. I felt, there, and there only, like a little king.

I always imagined Grampy with me, a little old baldheaded man with thick glasses. He was filled with folklore. I could ask him for advice at any moment; the king could ask his advisor for help with a nod of the head.

The king would pull open this drawer, that, and see what all his subjects were up to: the jar-counties full of Indian-head pennies ready to cater to his every need, the stamp-hinge envelop-lands waiting to rush off as his private emissaries, the plasticine territories neatly arranged and filled with delicate perforations, waiting to wait on him. All, all were at his beck and command, at his every swivel.

The room itself had a cavernous sense. A copy of the Magna Carta hung beside the door, middle-nineteenth century valentines under glass surrounded the doorway to the spacious walk-in storage closet, maps the size of tapestries depended from s-shaped, three-quarter-inch wide brass hooks secured by the top curve of the picture moulding.

The maps and charts I loved best of all. Those on the walls looked varnished, and the varnish had begun to crack. Grampy spoke of patinas. The thick wooden-knobbed doweling at the top or northern ends and at the southern bottoms made the maps look as though they were giant scrolls. Some of the maps were of the town where Grampy still lived, where my mom had been born, and had pictures of various houses and public buildings drawn down the sides and along the bottoms: the Seward Mansion, the State Prison, the Osborne House.

One map, a much smaller one, stayed spread out on the desk, under a piece of thick glass. Tiffany triangles of filigreed brass protected each corner. On this map I could lean and gaze for hours. At the bottom left it read, "Surveyed in 1842." And at the very bottom, to the right of the legend, I loved to read: "Published by the Director General at the Ordnance Survey Office, Phoenix Park, Dublin, 1847."

It was a map of Clear Island, County Cork, Ireland. Grampy explained to me about perches and chains and furlongs, about baronies and parishes and townlands, about contours and trigonometrical stations, about statute miles and spring tides and rights of way. But my grandfather, my visor, couldn't explain to me the exact nature of the marked antiquities. These sites held a special fascination for me, mainly because, at first, they appeared in a mysterious script I'd never before seen.

Grampy taught me how to use the *Encyclopedia Britannica*, the 1911 edition, in order to find things out. "School," he said, "is where you should learn to learn. That learned, the world's your oyster, boy." Under font, we discovered that the antiquities on the Ordnance Survey map were designated in Cloister Black. But I still didn't know what they were. Finally Grampy ordered an Irish-English dictionary: a Gallaun turned out to be a standing stone, and I decided I would not, after all, become a cartographer but an archaeologist.

End memory.'

End week-long workshop.

And the mighty little king, the budding archaeologist? Deghlan became a high school science teacher, and when his own children were grown and had left home, he and his wife finally had enough money to take vacations abroad. Sometimes they attended such seminars. But they also began to visit Ireland annually. Particularly Cape Clear Island, where they bought a cottage.

Cape had a quality he couldn't name, and he valued the island that much more for that. "True places," he remembered from Herman Melville, "are never on the map." And Cape, he felt, was full of "true places." The mystery he'd felt as a boy in the heavy Cloister Black script he experienced as a middle-aged man walking Cape. It wasn't just its isolation, the ruggedness of the terrain, the thoughtful little kindnesses of the people, the magic of its shifting light, the immediacy of all weathers; it felt well lived-in, like a comfy old slipper, but one that wouldn't wear out. At the same moment that he sensed people had been walking this hill, exploring that cave, for thousands of years, he also felt that no one, ever, had been here before now, on this rock, climbing this cliff. It was as though the universe was dramatising its age yet communicating itself as new-born.

One day, in early June of his fifty-ninth summer, already on Cape for his vacation, he had what seemed more than a waking dream. He heard the telephone ring, ring with strident urgency. He picked up the handset. The cradle shook. "Fitzgerald Park on the line: You are to come to our museum today. Without fail. It's time."

He knew it didn't happen, wasn't happening, not outside him. But it was happening nevertheless. He couldn't for the life of him refuse.

He left Cape on the nine o'clock ferry, journeyed to Baltimore on a flat sea, found his car, covered in dried salt, drove nonstop the hour and a half to Cork, exactly 59 miles on the odometer.

He had often seen the facsimile of the Cape Clear Stone in the island's Heritage Centre and, since he had also read book after book on the ancient Celts, Mother Goddesses, Druidism, Stonehenge, Newgrange, Pre-Christian Ireland, he knew that the time had more than come to see – to experience – the original stone. While he didn't like to leave the island, each day there precious, gale force wind or pea soup fog, he rationalised that he was going toward the island while leaving it. And he had no choice. Like the magical life-force of a giant in a fairy tale, Cape's secret heart beat on the second floor of a palace as good as on the other side of the world.

He spent the afternoon in Fitzgerald Park – all of it on the second floor of the museum.

The stone took him by surprise. It was nothing like the facsimile, which now was pure counterfeit, without texture, without dimensionality. Oh, he swung about with the fierce cosmological patterns – three swirling spirals, tra la, let the world be full of light, oh, and the fecundating circumscribing zigzags, bwa-zam, ka-boom. Straight on, Deghlan, straight on, world.

If Freud stood behind Leopold Bloom as he sat on Sandymount strand watching a sweet young thing, Jung, Deghlan imagined, stood behind him as he fantasised on the beginnings of this stone.

Where, he wondered, did the stone originate? A stone of such artistic power – and wasn't all art, Dada or La Tène or child's scribble, essentially religious in nature? – a stone of such soul-swirling had never been erected as mere decoration. A "decorated stone" my foot, he thought: five millennia back someone, someones, had a cause, had a conviction. Imagine having been an astronomer five thousand years ago. Imagine gathering the information necessary for an alignment. Hey, boy, hey, he thought, that's pre-pyramids!

Grampy, where are you? I need you.

On the way back to Baltimore he noticed he was all but in a meditation, a rambunctious meditation. And he had spoken that question, that declaration. In his mind or aloud, he couldn't tell. Like the phone ringing that morning.

And Grampy came. He held a cane in his hand, tap tap, and came hobbling down a quartz crystal lane toward where Deghlan stood. He said: "You're out in the big world now, Deghlan. Measure up: it's your chance."

"Huh?" was all he could utter. Then: "Grampy, I love you. How are you?"

"We know all that, Deghlan. I'm here because of what we don't know."

"It's been forty-two years."

"A year's but a wave upon the far shore."

"You always told me not to take love for granted."

"Deedles, that I'm here is love. Look for the sun, my son of my sun, my son of my daughter."

Deghlan swept his arms around his grandfather in an embrace of decades. His arms passed through the insubstantial old man, who winked mischievously, turned, hobbled off, tap tapping down the dazzling crystal path.

He pulled off the road. Tears streaming. He felt joyous; didn't know what had happened, but that it had happened at all was – was a fullness of being. He mumbled, "My cup runneth over in the presence."

Absorbing emotion, storing it up, treasure, he breathed loudly, deeply. Dilapidated cars, puffing tractors passed. Belching bus. Teetery trailer full of hay heading for barn, racing before clouds of black. The smell of pollen eased him back. He drove the bends into Skibbereen, around the narrow twists and turns to Baltimore. He parked across from the Garda Station out of habit, and walked as if in a daze to the waiting mailboat, its propellers already sending out swirls into the harbour.

His grandfather. Measure up. Big chance. The sun.

Yes, the sun. He would take careful measurements; would haunt the tomb winter solstice sunset, summer solstice sunrise, would eat and drink at the tomb, eat and drink the tomb. If the tomb had an orientation, the stone had a home.

With a mission, he felt free. Had no need to make choices. All was given. You don't have to study archaeology to love a stone. Study kills beloveds. Hawthorne's young doctor cutting out the birthmark of his Desdemona wife, foul birthmark rooted deep, in purity of soul. Study does away with wisdom. What's wisdom anyway but small kindnesses done.

Crossing Roaringwater Bay to the island, he went further than he'd ever gone. He let himself go, travelled with the speed of light. He entered the world of stone, imagined himself stone. Sailing out to Cape, he became stone, the stone.

Stone-crossed mind. Stone-swirling mind. I'm on my back in 1874, lying where the marauders left me three thousand years ago when they savaged my mom. They dragged me away, a slave, and then discarded me in that long narrow field. Tom Shipsey's island townland, Croha West, oh you Dónal O Síocháin, you Pádraig O Ríogáin, you cleared the field, you found me, you cared for my beauty. You carried me to that sonless priest and he planted me in his kitchen garden and I bloomed. He left. I withered.

I've been abducted, evicted, abandoned, centuries, millennia of neglect. Give me back Cnoc Caraintín. Give me back my mother, all our mothers. You poor people, believing in one god, masculine. It takes two, male and female you should recognise as they them. Nothing's wrong with you except imbalance. Imbalance leads you to deny creation joy. When you then become arrogant, repressive, negative, so too does your god. Monotheism sucks. Masculinity unlimited. Marry off your Jehovah, your Allah; and as you regain your balance, so too your world.

How dare they designate me a symbol of social cohesion, an expression of territorial behaviour in small-scale sedentary societies? I'm simply a place for light, loving light, to rest, to reveal the mere structure of the world, the order, that which gives cohesion to flocks of floating souls. That which affirms the cycle of birth and death and rebirth and redeath.

I was a centre, a meeting place, a loved one now and then in light.

I was the clitoris, the touch of masculine in the feminine place. I watched my father the sun enter my mother the earth's straight and narrow chamber.

> Sperm light, sperm bright,
> thou guidest my soul
> through all the dark nights.

Whoa, boy. Deghlan disembarked. He didn't extend his greeting to those around him on the pier. He couldn't: he didn't see them. Yet he walked as deliberately as a man can walk. Each stride became part of sacred journey. Toward light.

When he reached the foot of the highest hill, he didn't hesitate, didn't falter. He climbed over the initial stile. The tractor-rutted, twisting road to the windmills might have been as flat as the pavement before the Taj Mahal. He couldn't stop. Were they the furies behind him? No matter.

Roaringwater Bay filled with gentle red. The sun sank into the sea, and when it had disappeared, a residue of clarity bathed the mountains of West Cork as though they had just been created. But Deghlan wasn't one for sunsets just then but one for stones.

As he examined yet again the prehistoric tomb, the sub-circular spread of stone, he concentrated on its centre. There lay a modest, three-sided chamber. He sat, leaned back against the side facing north by northeast. Before him, not ten feet away, was a small row of five stones pointing in the same direction. They'd always been there and he'd never seen them before. Now if, he thought, if the orientation was on the summer solstice sunrise, then we could be certain that this site is indeed a passage tomb. Passage tombs have decorated stones. I'll sleep here every night around the summer solstice until I see what I see.

He lay back. And he slept through the night. And woke, dew drenched, stiff, hungry for the sun. The sky to the east was brightening.

He was atop his favourite hill in the world. He checked his watch: a little after 04:00 on 06 20 93. A dawning before him. He stretched, stood, stretched again, sat, wriggled his back against the back of the chamber. He pulled out the compass he had started carrying with him and once more read the orientation: 40 degrees east of north. The stones stretched out before him. Chamber sides? Marker stones? The horizon glowed, became glowing gold. A line of poetry came to him, a point of reference, "Gold to airy thinness beate." Before him he felt the horizon of the world. Throbbing. He was ready. He was, he felt, at the end of a long tunnel.

And like celestial clockwork, at last, there it was, in a cloudless golden dawn: on the horizon 5 miles NNW of Rosscarbery, in the gap formed by Carrigfadda – the highest hill the east had to offer – and Carrigagrenane; there, in the valley between the two hills, in line with the passage and shining into the chamber, rose the solstice sun, manifesting himself in the lowest point of the gap. Twenty-two miles from Cnoc Caraintín, the gap perfectly framed the emergent disk.

Deghlan could hear faint cheers from Fitzgerald Park.

Home of stone, stone home.

He felt as if he had been plucked up by the ankles, held aloft in the trembling air, and spanked with beauty.

The media briefly took over, had their field day, left. The sadly pilfered but panoramic site would enter the archaeological tomes, as would Deghlan, who began to wonder if he hadn't become responsible for all future pilfering. Would his discovery of what he loved, he wondered, contribute to its timeless destruction?

He went on. The site acquired implications, national, international. National, because the tomb became the first authenticated passage tomb in County Cork, the third in all of Ireland with summer solstice alignment. International, because the discovery buttressed the growing belief that all such tombs have astronomical orientations. Had he helped, had he been helped, he mused, to help the world regain a millimetre of balance?

Are picturesque site, modest tomb, early occupant earlier or contemporary with "earliest" Newgrange? Hang on, pal. Could Mr Stone's passage tomb be the earliest astronomical site in the world? But that way lies inflation. The other, pedantry. Careful.

The night he had that thought, he had a dream: His grandfather, holding a cane in one hand, tap tap, came hobbling down a quartz crystal lane toward where Deghlan stood. A rising sun shone bars of light along the lane, striking Deghlan. They shone straight through the body of his grandfather, warmed Deghlan's chest. His grandfather came up to him, raised his free hand to Deghlan's brow, said simply: "Son of my son, you could do worse in this world than spend your little time and energy, as the ancients did, to orient yourself properly. Passage tombs are but metaphors reminding us of heavenly homes, eternal directions." He flung his cane to the four winds, wrapped his strong arms around Deghlan's chest. They embraced. His grandfather had youthful muscles, stone hard. Chest to chest they stood, his grandfather as warm as a stone that has soaked up the sun's rays through millennia. And then the sun set. And Deghlan was in a large house, his own, with a deep, cavernous cellar, filled with barrel-vaulted chambers he'd never before seen.

He awoke. He felt ready to chart new regions. At breakfast he said to his wife, "Anyone for cartography of the soul?" She looked at him. He looked at her. She waited. He waited. And then, out poured miles, days, years of laughter, laughter that spread around them, laughter in which they could take their ease, laughter that was like welcoming, warm, hummocky, multifoliate grass in which they rolled apart, together. The world, to them both, felt new, they new to the world.

Looking back once again, Deghlan winced, caught himself thinking, "Somethin' to be said for tunnel vision."

God's Spy

Late one blustery September afternoon, the harbour wash already sounding an ominous, guttural roar, Connie and his dad rounded up the flock of forty-two sheep – with Connie playing the part of the missing sheep dog. Up and down the headlands he scrambled, sometimes having to sprint along barely discernible rabbit tracks while hoping he'd not land in the mouth or backdoor of a burrow. Occasionally he had to leap through a patch of shin-prickly gorse to keep wayward ewe, rambunctious ram, or spooked lamb from breaking out of his wildly gestured shouted parameters and leading the others helter-skelter astray, perhaps panicking lemming style over cliff. By the time father and son had herded the last of the stragglers down the hill home, into the crush, and hooked the galvanised gate shut with a u-shaped piece of thick wire, Connie discovered he was drenched with sweat, panting as if at halftime of a college football match, and worried that the desperate part lay dead ahead.

Instinctively he'd come to dread the ritual yet essential dip to renew protection from fly strike and all those consequent creepy-crawly maggots that seemed to him to delight in delving into innocent flesh. With almost every sheep emerging from the end of the crush into the ground-level, four-foot-deep tank, Connie had to lean way over from the concrete side of the dip, grab an ear, or a handful of fleece, and, for all his worth, pull the flustered creature those critical five feet until hooves again touched earth and the soaked sheep could bound away, free to roam the headlands once more.

But the splash. The acrid chemical stink. How, he wondered, had he forgotten to stuff into his back pocket those elbow-length rubber gloves that hung from a beam in the calf house? How had he forgotten that look of panic in the eyes of the bucking splashing sheep, that look that had followed him off the island all the pot-holed windy way to Cork, that–

"Well done, son!" his father exclaimed.

Connie felt a full slap on the back, heard a long exhale. "No bother, dad," he lied.

"Time for tea."

"Naw, a walk."

"After the miles you've run?"

"To get it out of my system."

"The herding?"

"The inhuman dipping. The fear that's in 'em. They act as though they're swimming for their lives."

"They are. In the long run."

"Well, I feel as though I've been after torturing them."

"For their own good."

"No good in it. Why can't we spray or paint 'em with the preventative? Treat 'em gently, humanely? As if they were children?"

"Son, be careful of that old imagination of yours. It could lead ye astray so."

"Well, why can't we?"

"It's too expensive, too time-consuming."

"Okay, okay, you're right, as always, dad," – he couldn't keep his disgruntled sarcasm to himself – "and that's why I'm going to skip tea and take a walk. Straighten my imagination out. Keep it from leaping protective boundaries."

"Good man. And you might want oilskins. Looks like one mighty squall there out to sea. Not far off, neither. This wind must be gusting fifty knots an hour. Watch them drawstrings don't snap into no eyeball."

"Right so, dad. See ya later. Be home by sunset. Eight-thirty or thereabouts. Slán."

"Slán agat."

In the front hallway of the family farmhouse – full of his ancestors since the middle 1800s – Connie donned the oilskins, changed from wellies into hiking boots, by habit – despite his twenty-two years – let his mum know what he was about, and that he was skipping tea, and set off. The wash below now sometimes thundered, what his granddad had always said a warning sign: no fishing for three days, or else.

Connie decided he'd head for the southwesternmost headland of the island, an area free from any trace of mankind, a drystone-wall-and-fence-free few acres where not even sheep or goats grazed. Rabbits galore, yes, even a booming colony – the sandy soil made burrowing easy – but nothing farmed. The jagged cliffs – handy refuge for rabbits under threat – closed in from both sides, the land narrowing into slender stony spit.

Walking the upper lake road, Connie found himself reviewing his recent life. A mere year before he'd been debating whether to become a Man of God and transfer to Maynooth. Thanks to his paternal grandmother, who'd taught herself to read at the age of sixty-three and would select a story from either the Bible or the collected works of the Brothers Grimm every night before the fire, and read aloud for a pure ten to fifteen minutes, he'd come to enjoy exploring the mythologies of the world, and the Bible, Old and New, and had become particularly fascinated by the differences between those who were good and those who were evil, between what constitutes the differences between good and evil. The more he read about Jesus, the more he liked him, and his parables – to him the real miracles – but the more he read about Christ, the more he doubted him. John seemed wish-fulfilling fiction, Luke biographical fact. And when, with his fine-tooth comb, he tried to ferret out biblical justification for the celibacy of priests, and for their having to be men, he began to doubt his organised religion's base. Still, he came to value Jesus as a contrarian. The Sermon on the Mount he felt an ignored moral watershed: "Unto him that smiteth thee on the one cheek offer also the other." Tell that, he thought, to the Rev. Ian Paisley, or born-again George W.

One morning last spring, as an experiment, he'd walked the length of Cork city's Grand Parade and Western Road looking every person coming toward him in the eye – if they let him – and sending out heart-felt health and love to each soul regardless of age or sex, colour or condition. Some smiled, some turned away, some ignored him, three asked for money. He knew he hadn't learned anything, except that to be overtly loving could be construed as being forward, even a rude invitation, and he didn't want to add to the number of those.

That afternoon, in a used bookstore not far from UCC, he chanced upon a detailed account of what had happened in the Nazi concentration camps. Impulsively he bought Primo Levi's *If This Is A Man*, took it straight to a quiet spot under a tree beside the River Lee, read it cover to cover that afternoon, and had to conclude then and there that, though God there was, surely, just look at the miracle of new-born lamb, or see the Milky Way as but a minor galaxy, His Nibs was unfortunately not full of love for each and every individual. Levi may have made it through his concentration camp, but what a way home. And all those years later, the suicide, the belated consequence of what he'd experienced? Maybe, heaven forfend, a divine plan could be said to lie behind the death of Levi, and the tortured deaths of the Jews and gypsies, though that lacked all logical sense; but to talk about an all-loving, personal, caring God when one-and-a-half million Jewish children alone were murdered in a handful of years, well, where was the ubiquitous all-loving Almighty then? On vacation in some other fairytale universe?

So Connie'd elected to stick with his concentration in philosophy and, to his parent's dismay, quit attending Mass. And to his own disquiet, too much of what he saw, whether walking the streets of Cork, or helping his dad dunk the sheep in the dip, reminded him of his interpretation of part of Kant's Categorical Imperative: when you treat even a single human being, even an evil human being, like an object, you commit evil. He recognised that he'd been treating those sheep as objects. Okay, he admitted, they're not human beings, no way, and the dip's for their own good, all the way, but still, I saw their eyes as they went through the dip. Their eyes had been human, had become beseeching, desperate. Their eyes had been screaming. And yes, dad, so's my imagination.

A rain-filled squall struck him head-on. He had to turn his face aside – and walk, hood up, with the right side of his head and body butting into the wind like the bow of a boat into waves. And then he saw her, all ninety-one years of her, the oldest woman of the island, the so-called island queen. He knew the stories about her, how she hadn't been off the island for over forty-five years, how her husband died tragically at sea only a few years after they'd married, she still childless; how she'd become as stubborn in her ways – he smiled at his change of her sex – as a rutting bull. But what was Ita doing out in this storm, she close to being but a bundle of brittle thin sticks? He imagined her scooped up by the wind and blown away to the Scillies – if not to Kingdom Come.

The skies opened. Connie hunkered down beside a drystone wall, feeling as if a spy truly wet behind the ears. And then it came back to him, the existential King Lear imaginatively, even lyrically, calling himself and his daughter Cordelia "God's spies", at last reunited spies that are to take upon themselves "the mystery of things" once they've entered prison. Tragedy – he questioned – could you be ruthless without irony?

Before him, two small pastures away, he watched not the king and his soon dead daughter but the aged childless queen hobble her way toward a small field with a single cow in it, saw she carried a bucket in one hand, a cane in the other. The panoramic landscape, dozens of walled pastures, a few house ruins, a few empty sheds, the sea behind them all, and but one creature moving. The juxtaposition turned his immediate world into a stage. Despite downpour and gusting wind, Ita slowly, awkwardly climbed over the stile into the field, approached the cow, knelt on the ground beside the cow's hind legs, placed the bucket under her udder, began milking. Out in the open. One single soul, a dark blue and red kerchief over her head, her forehead sometimes leaning against the cow's flank. No raingear. He could see Ita's knobbly hands gripping the teats, pulling and squeezing. The well-trained cow didn't budge. He thought, Beckett, are you in the wings? I'm watching your theatre of the absurd. To God. Godot. To Dog. Holy Cow.

After a few minutes, or fifteen – Connie wasn't certain – Ita finished the twice daily chore, struggled over the stile and, cane in right hand, bucket in left, started limping for home. Twice gusts caught her, drove her tiny humped self backward a few tottering steps, the pail acting like a wind-sock, but she didn't fall or falter and, gust past, started immediately to navigate what remained of the painful hundred yards back to her cottage. And disappeared from sight. He wanted to clap, to witness an encore. And he understood the truth to the stories about her pastures not having gates. When she moved her pet, she'd first remove stone after stone in a new pasture, open a gap, and only then dismantle a section of the old pasture – and herd her friend to fresh grass. Then she'd rebuild the stones, eventually closing both gaps.

Connie remained kneeling in the lee of the wall. After another squall had run its course, he rose. Instead of continuing his walk to the fringe of the island, he turned toward home, a spring in his step, the wind at his back, a needed new parable in his private bible. He wished Primo Levi could have been with him at that altar of the earth. He looked forward to helping his dad with the sheep next summer and – they'd be about sitting down right now – to having tea with his parents tonight.

God's Backside

He knew exactly where he was, physically. Not only on land but on water. And he'd no need of any navigational fix. Anchored four hundred yards east-northeast of the looming Fastnet Rock and hooking six mackerel as fast as he could remove the previous six from his feathers and toss his heavily-weighted line over the gunwale again, Jamesy still wondered where he was, where he was going, what he could do for his father. Past him winged skeins of gannets, low-flying shearwater, the occasional darting storm petrel, the swallow of the sea – and all seemed to have relaxed purpose.

The tidal race roughened the surface water, made a slight crackling sound. As if the sea debated becoming a mighty river in spate. He was reminded of what the top lid of Davy Jones' locker must sound like. But, hey, boyo, eight boxes in two hours. "One cute fox," crossed his mind. Still, he felt lost for all that – and prayerless, without the good word.

Somehow mackerel no longer had anything to do with him. Nor pollack, hake, herring. Nor monkfish, sole, plaice. Nor the good money he made from them. Nor the upwelling of fabled nutrients a little further out beside the Continental Shelf. Somehow this fisherman life seemed selfish, introspective, wasn't him any longer. While he knew he fished well, and supported faithfully his mother and younger siblings from the money he made, he wasn't – much as he felt a man of the sea – a fisherman. Not in spirit. Not now. Not with the war going on.

And he ached, not from putting his back into oars, not from pulling up line after tugging line, but from feeling lost, like a fish out of water. Him, twelve generations back his blood went on the island. Minimum. That O'Driscoll pirate blood in there too. Back and back. Probably back to the Celts. To *St Ciarán*'s forbears – himself the eldest of the four pre-Patricians. Yes, he loved to have Father Donal bless the *Maire Cait* with spring water from the saint's holy well on his Feastday, March 5th, loved the ridiculous reassurance that she was unsinkable for yet another year, but right now Jamesy felt like a blow-in both on and around his home island, little Oileán Chléire, its O'Driscoll Castle of Gold showing faintly there to the northeast, good old Dún an Oir. Yes, a blow-in, a bird picked up by a hurricane and dropped down a wild time later on a continent unknown. Not another member of his species within two thousand miles.

What to do with himself, that was the question. He wasn't only a bird off course, he decided, but one without any sense of direction. In fact, in truth – and he was beginning to realise a gulf (larger than the stream he knew so well) existed between the two – the war made him feel a dispossessed person. Him a DP. Yet him at home. But, dear God, if – if, if, if, he pondered while he unhooked the flopping mackerel – if he left to volunteer his energies to the Irish Republican Army, why, his family'd famish. Couldn't sacrifice them just to give himself the right perch, the right flight pattern. A bird don't forsake its young, no, it feeds 'em no matter.

When he finished filling the ninth box, his last, he debated motoring to Baltimore, decided he'd get there not as fast but with more pleasure, more connection, maybe, if he raised sail and went with the wind, what Father Donal called God's breath, some Hebrew word behind it, and Jamesy loved words. For some reason he couldn't fathom he recognised that he felt better, indeed, thought better, came up with phrases better, when under press of sail rather than when dependent on this new phenomenon called horsepower. What he nicknamed donkeypower.

Before he hoisted his inherited maroon sail, he peered up at the Fastnet. Sure but it knew what it was doing. Standing there, tough, purposeful, at graceful ease no matter war, hurricane, rogue wave. He'd seen the tower – viewed it from Cape – sometimes totally submerged, all hundred eighty-plus feet of it disappearing into breaking seas. Man, some rocks go down and down. And man alive, how some reemerge – and some words, some people too.

Sail up, safely luffing, a petrel deftly swerving, missing the tip of his boom, he raised anchor from off the edge of his favourite reef, some sixty feet down, that chasm beside it dropping another hundred and twenty feet, more, down into what he privately called the Territory of the Rich Fish. Darting back to the stern, and thinking petrel storm petrel while he did so, he grabbed the main sheet and tiller and swiftly swung his bow north. The sail's belly puffed, banged out full. He paid out sheet until the boom strained at right angles to the hull. The sound of wake rising, his arm looped over the tiller, reassured him. But he wondered if Baltimore was his real destination. Not his soul's destination, ridiculous, too much to contemplate. But his spirit's. And as he peered across Roaring Water Bay, two dolphins arced playfully not twenty feet from his boat. Again and again they appeared, swimming in tandem. West, young men and women, boys and girls, go west.

The next day Jamesy woke to the sound of wind rustling thatch and the sudden thought, like a rare match struck before first light to reignite the kitchen fire, that the coming day, someday, will be a long time ago. Here he was, all twenty-two years of him, a corporation of a man – or so proudly proclaimed by his mum – and the rest of the brood, four younger brothers and six younger sisters, in the room with him, packed like fish. He thought of salted pilchard in a hogshead home. To take a leak meant stepping over bodies in the dark before stepping outside – or putting the bucket to use by kneeling down beside it and letting loose down its side so that no noise woke a sibling. Yes, he could, he must, do something more than fish to help, father or no father, Reign of Terror or no Reign of Terror – and those blasted Auxillary Forces who'd arrested his da for "terrorist offences".

What dangerous act or crime had his father ever committed? he asked. No more crime on 'im than on a child in the cradle. He'd just kept a passing gunrunner from drowning. Why, he'd been a valued Lightkeeper at the Fastnet Lighthouse from 1914 to 1917. The only Cape Clear Islander ever so to be. So of course Jamesy knew the ins and outs of the place not only from his recent boyhood excursions there with his da, not only from of late providing the English keepers the occasional fish. Gratis as the air God gives us, too. Yes, maybe he'd join the Schull Company of the Irish Republican Army after all, having said no a month back, but he'd make it clear he'd be for duty around home as much as possible. They'd have to let him keep fishing.

Under cover the way to go, the way those dolphins yesterday had suddenly disappeared, never shown themselves again for as long as he watched. But then, who wasn't under cover? Even his Auntie Margot – and he was honoured to have been confided in by her – had joined the Cumnann na Mban, that group of women who knew as much about smart spying as a conger does about the bottom of the sea.

Why, it wasn't but three weeks back he'd taken his squeeze-box out to the lighthouse to play for a party. He'd piloted six of his closest friends there in his twenty-three-foot boat – this time without sail – landed them safely, secured a stern rope to the iron landing ring, and moored his craft thirty feet out from the closest rock. Then he operated the lighthouse crane, lifted the three young women off his boat in a giant basket, them shrieking in a wild mix of glee and fear. And didn't they dance. Didn't the English keepers get a kick out of the illegality, to say nothing of Betsy's antics. Jesus Mary and Joseph but she could dance. And the ankles on her. And that lightning mind. Her words. One day. This Godless war ever over.

But today now, up since dawn, Jamesy had a serious predicament. Twelve men from the mainland town of Schull had landed on Cape the previous night, the seas too high for them to complete their mission. Their leader, Roger, called on Jamesy. This flock weren't no birds off course.

Together Roger and Jamesy sauntered off Sean Duffy's pier, where Jamesy'd been tying new leaders and hooks onto his long-line, three hundred hooks spread out over a mile of line.

"Every six yards I tie a leader," he was explaining, "with just that touch less line strength so that if a hook snags, the leader rather than the line gives, breaks. Ye've got to think that way."

"That's like us, Jamesy," said the fatherly Roger. "If one of us gets caught, he's got to break in such a way that no one else is hurt. The I.R.A. comes first, the individuals that make it up come second."

"Yes, yes. I understand."

They gestured as though they were talking weather, fishing, male jokes. But they had carefully established distance so that no one could eavesdrop.

"Jamesy, you've heard how we're turning the tide against the Crown Forces, how our skirmish at Kilmichael taught the R.I.C. a lesson or two?" The young man nodded. "And we're blowin' up their lorries and armoured cars. Last week we got one a mile outside Drimoleague. They're gettin' scared. But we're running out of explosives."

"I'm afraid you won't find any here on Cape."

"No, no, no. Listen, we've heard a leak. We suspect we know where there's a right store of 'em."

"No."

"Will you join us? The Schull Battalion?"

"That an invitation?"

"We don't twist arms – until you're one of us," Roger chuckled. "Yes," he continued. "And you're the boyo who knows how to land us on the Fastnet no matter the weather – or the time of day . . . or night!"

"The Fastnet?"

"You heard me."

Roger looked hard at Jamesy before winking.

"Could you take my men there in your boat, Jamesy? Tonight? I've heard all about your recent visits. I'll take our boat back to Schull after this meeting, all in order. No suspicions. The others got aboard my *Golden Fort* at Gun Point after I left the harbour coming here, well, we were going to raid the Fastnet last night, but conditions became too rough. Anyway, to the people on the mainland we're not even here, I'm just out to sea again."

"Gelignite on the Fastnet?" said Jamesy, as if speculating aloud. "The tear-drop, the most prominent spot in all West Cork, a secret site for munitions?" He was talking to himself.

"You know how to land there at night. How to grab that iron ring. How many times have ye done the deed?"

"A dozen. Maybe fifteen. Don't know. Plenty."

"At night's something else and ye've done it then?" asked Roger.

"Yes."

"The keepers, they know you, right?"

"Yes."

"So you stay with the boat, and the rest will surprise the keepers, two can keep 'em under control, tie 'em up and blindfold 'em. And the nine empty the storeroom. We know how to work cranes too – and your boat can hold two tons?"

"One, one and a half. Yes. If no significant swell. And there isn't much today."

"Well?"

"Nothing I'd rather do, be. I'm a member? And can go on living here on Cape?"

"You're a member – and we'll put you to the test tonight. Make a man of ya. You've a full tank? With reserves?"

"Yes."

"And you could land the gang at Gun Point afterwards and be home to Cape before first light? That is, if you leave the Fastnet by two a.m."

Jamesy looked out to sea, saw three herring gulls beating past, said, "It's new moon tonight, which I'm sure ye know." Roger gave his friendly wink. "And it's summer solstice time, so it's light until a good eleven, not pitch black until midnight. We leave then?"

"You got it."

"I'll moor this afternoon alongside the Bull's Nose. After dinner I'll depart as for fishing, make plenty of noise going out."

"Everything matters, Jamesy."

"The speed of the spring tide too," mused Jamesy, then said briskly, "You've a hiding place ready for the explosives?"

"Ready and waiting. Leave it to me. A bunker in the most innocent of places. All but under noses. Ask no more. Just get my men and the materiel to Gun Point after you've done the deed."

"Rock, here we come."

Roger solemnly shook hands with Jamesy.

"I'm a member?"

"A member of the Irish Republican Army in good standing or sitting. No ifs, ands, or buts so."

"Roger, one question. Do you know if my father did any more than rescue that gunrunner before being arrested, incarcerated, solitary confinement?"

"No, but I know" – he placed his patriarchal arm over Jamesy's shoulders – "that everything we see and can't understand – all them twisted knots of our behaviour – them's is God's backside."

"Ouch. That hurts." Roger removed his arm, giving a few pats as he did so. Jamesy added slowly, "Bollocks, but that helps too. God's backside. Yes," he mused, "everything can't be face to face, heart to heart. Thanks, Roger," he added, looking straight into the eyes. "And now an idea."

"Shoot."

"You leave with the men. Then, if any word ever gets out, which I doubt, given the solid Republican nature of my neighbours, you've all gone, left Cape lot, stock, and barrel. You motor past the castle, on to that point with two caves tucked back around it. You know the one. Go into the first one, the outer one – it's plenty deep for the likes of your boat – drop off your crew, and get on home with ye. That way you'll all have left here – and you arrive home just as you left home and no one the wiser. Late evening, nightfall, after a string of lobsters, I'll poke in there, pick up the lads – and in there they're out of sight to anyone at sea or on Cape – I've never known anyone but me even go in there – and, pitch dark, we set off for the Fastnet. How 'bout that?"

"That's why we want you aboard – and piloting your boat, and being knacky not just with words but with ropes," replied Roger.

Mid-afternoon, the twelve mainlanders walked unescorted back to North Harbour, untied the moorings for the *Golden Fort*, pulled the fenders aboard, and purred out of the harbour, nodding to a few local lads on the pier. Roger explained to his men how essential it was for him and the *Golden Fort* to return home, be visibly present in church at 11 o'clock Mass the next morning. Maybe they could be there too. It would be an alibi for them all, for, he being innocent, and his boat in the day before, they were all innocent.

To be on the safe side, once well outside North Harbour, all but Roger slowly sank out of sight. Ten minutes later he nosed his boat into the cove known as An Fhaill Mhór, and on gingerly into the cave Jamesy had designated. The eleven had no trouble jumping onto a ledge, where, with slabs of bread they'd coated with lard and ham while underway, twelve revolvers, and four bullets each, they'd wait. And, just in case, should anything happen to Jamesy in the meantime and he have to leave them stranded, Roger'd come back the following afternoon.

After dinner, telling his mother not to worry if he was late, Jamesy strode to the harbour, gunned his engine twice before casting off, and departed North Harbour, the *Maire Cait* at full throttle before he passed the Bull's Nose. Out from the Stacks he swung northeast, felt as though he was going into another world even as he avoided the treacherous Óglach region, which he knew like the back of his hand. Soon he was hauling a short string of fifteen lobster pots close to Bird Island. He reset the pots with some ripe rabbit meat, shot them in almost the same place as before, tossed his catch of five lobsters into a holding cage having tied their claws shut, and headed west into yet more of this known but unknown world, dusk falling fast.

The harder he tried not to think of the forty-seven armed Marines at the Schull Coastguard Station, forty-five minutes across the bay, the louder their alarm bell went off in his imagination. Finally, through the almost fully fallen darkness, he called out to them, six miles away, "Come and get me. Try it. I'll lead you between rocks you won't even know are there – until it's too late." He laughed aloud, seeing them flounder. And in his mind their alarm bell fell silent.

Under engine only, hand light on the tiller, he powered past the castle, past the rock known as Tón Loinge, or Ship's Bottom, and, rounding the point, began edging his way toward the mouth of the cave. In a series of quick reverses and forward shifts, he held the boat steady, his eyes getting used to the hole of utter darkness ahead. He wondered if it was the gaping maw of hell, wondered what would happen if some surprise rogue wave decided to pay a visit, and then again he laughed aloud: he could feel more than see the presence of the men there, perched like nesting gulls. He shifted forward ever so gently, moved ahead half a yard, slipped into reverse, slowly made his way to within three feet of the ledge. Holding her there, hoping, he called out, "Jump two at once, every time the boat's close to the peak of her rise. Grab the stays as you swing aboard. Now!"

In no time the eleven were aboard – only Tim slipped into the sea, but grabbed the gunwale first and quickly hauled himself back in – and Jamesy was reversing out into the cove, a few waves pouring over the transom, but no matter. He turned the *Maire Cait*, headed through the choppy seas below the cliffs.

Black midnight it was. Except for the swivelling lighthouse beam. Jamesy, to his complete surprise, felt good, felt found. He could feel a gift of grin widening up to his ears as he had the men spread their weight evenly on both sides of his boat.

"We'll motor another half a mile, then cut back on the engine, make ourselves quiet as a marauding mink," said Jamesy to the fellows closest to him. "Wind's perfect, from the east. Always knew the east wind had to have some good in it. We'll just glide in to the loading area–"

"Look there. Searchlight. Christ, it's coming this way."

"British patrol boat."

"Circling the Fastnet."

"And we're just cruising around the Bill of Cape," said Jamesy, having already given the *Maire Cait* a southeastern direction of innocence.

"Just what we wanted. Seriously. Now we know where she is – and if she doesn't spot us, she'll not be back for a good three hours," whispered Michael. "Normally. I've been watching her manoeuvers for weeks now. Never know when she's first going to appear, but after you've got those hours of grace."

"Grace it is, lads. See? She's heading for the Mizen so. Let's start countdown now. How far, Jamesy? Four miles?"

"Three and a half now."

"Twenty minutes?"

"Up sail. We've a perfect following wind. That's it, pull that halyard. Tight. Cleat her there. Watch your heads now. Hard a-lee," cried Jamesy, letting the boom swing abruptly from port to starboard, the sail bellying. He throttled down a notch, the engine quieting to a barely discernible hum. And he had the strangest sensation, as if he knew exactly, down to the very inch, where he was in a world in which he'd never been. On course. Straight ahead. Straight toward the Fastnet Rock. Straight toward the destination that would do the most for effecting the freedom of his father. With the swathe of the Fastnet light passing overhead every five seconds, he saw himself a grey heron, slow wings propelling him along to the very perch he sought prior to nabbing his prey. He a grey heron preparing to stab, a grey heron on the nightly prowl not far from home.

"Lads, when we're there, ten minutes left, I want Michael to lower stern anchor when I give the word, pay out the rope until we're right up to within jumping distance of the iron ring. I know, we might not be able to see the ring exactly, but I've jumped for it before. At night too. With a rope around my waist–"

"You can't see your hand in front of your face. You can't do that. Isn't there a ledge like in the cave?"

"Just that ring. No ledge. And when I get it–"

"If you get it."

"When I get it, we'll be there, ropes fast, all swarm ashore on a little boom just for that purpose."

"The keepers?"

"Two'll probably be asleep, the other up in the tower, way up at the top of the spiral staircase."

"You get us there, Jamesy, secure us there, we've practiced the rest, know the sleeping quarters, the stairs, the room at the top, how to dismantle the wireless. You work the boom, then the crane; you men, you know your duties: who's to watch over the two off duty, who's to march the keeper on duty to the other two, the four to load the basket, the three to offload the crane. If we're lucky, it'll take three, maybe four hours before someone comes to the keepers' rescue, probably that patrol boat – and we've left nary a trace. We'll be on the mainland, in Church, and Jamesy, you home, tidying up your poor catch before bed."

The iron ring, that was all Jamesy could think of as he headed toward the northeast corner of the Fastnet. He remembered slowly every jump he'd made for it. But never in a swell the size of this one. The wind had freshened that bit since leaving Cape, and the swell, well, it was always higher at the Fastnet than on Cape, two to three feet higher. Could be a six-foot rise and fall. Yes, with a rope around his waist, a revolver in his pocket, and, please God, his heron talons at the ready, he'd go for it.

Engine quiet; stern anchor down and fast, no drag; rope being paid out; Jamesy gave the tiller to fellow fisherman Alex, and walked the narrow side-deck to the bow, where he waited. Waited. The engine was now off, the sail lowered, the ring ten feet off, nine, eight. He peered through the darkness, the now slightly starlit base of the little island before him. He was rising, falling, rising, falling, and believed that touch of glint there – it had to be – didn't it? – the ring. Up and up and up. From his perch, he leapt, heart sideways. With his heron self, he stabbed. And it was cold, and it was solid. A wave washed over his head, a hump of ocean, and he clung there, thrust the rope through the ring as another wave washed over, had it tied before the next, the boat made fast, the boat suspended safely between anchor and ring. He scrambled up onto safe stone, swung out a boom for the men to grab, be swung ashore. No noise, no squeaking of cogs. While he was a bit bocketty at the knees, and dripping, in five minutes all the men save three were on the Fastnet and swarming silently toward their duties. The ten-foot steel door to the lighthouse wasn't locked, the single keeper was fully surprised, offered no resistance. They yanked three tubes from the wireless, rendered it useless. The three keepers – the man on duty having been marched below from his bright post – face down on the floor of the sleeping quarters, were blindfolded, trussed as tight as if they'd been pigs before a slaughter that never came.

All together, seventeen cartons of guncotton, three of primers and detonators, two of ammunition, and fifty-three rifles were swung out to the *Maire Cait* in the crane's net basket. Roughly a ton of spoils. And they were off one and a half hours later.

Engine full throttle all the way to the mainland, Jamesy dropped the eleven off at Gun Point at three-thirty-seven – according to the only watch aboard – arrived back in North Harbour as first light began to illumine the scene. He berthed the *Maire Cait*, dropped the lobster holding cage into the harbour, tied it up alongside two others, coiled and stowed the extra ropes, cleaned up a few scraps of evidence from certain cartons. He didn't know what was next, be it tuna on the long-line or Crown Forces on the short, but he knew he'd deal with it as best he could. So despite what human beings do to fellow human beings that they cannot comprehend, the grey heron folded his wings and waited.

Gas Man

For Joel ben Izzy, who saw Jonah's friend & lived to tell of it

From the kitchen garden Diarmuid spied it, a short solitary stretch of thick tannish-white foam heaving with barely discernible swells right at the mouth of the inner harbour. He rubbed his eyes. Looked again. No, no foam line, no apparition. A curious hump in the hump of sea.

"Stop," he exclaimed.

Last night had been what Ciarán, his Boston-based big brother, had learned him to call a 'wing doozy'. Anne-Marie, no, ouch, she weren't speakin' t' him again. He'd heard nothing but battened-down silence in the steamy kitchen, watched trickly runnels of moisture inside the single-glazed windows to the south. He'd raised his knife and fork upright, his freckled fists either side of his place, but she'd taken his gesture literally, had bustled brusquely about, as if to say she was after fitting his breakfast in amongst her rosary of main chores – caring for three B&Bers in the dining room, organising dinner, placing the grocery order by phone with the mainland supermarket, and preparing martyr-like the mixture of Sow Breeder and table scraps for the saddleback pigs – and here it was going on eleven, Jesus Mary and Joseph.

When she'd turned on the Pat Kenny show, he knew she'd roll away from him that night too. Ships passing. Hoot hoot. Long Fastnet foghorn hoots. Eerie, relationship. Tangled fishlines. Longlines at that. Sometimes you just have to cut bait. But they don't teach you that in school, not here, not then. Just inform youse like the church, don't, don't, don't. How to untangle, you God, you goddamn God you.

He could suddenly not remember what her inner thigh looked like, felt like, once white as pollack flesh, smooth as a buoy at sea. Fourteen years married. Sure but he might as well, tonight, go out. Bloody hell but a chat in the pub's people, a night at home's TV. But not for more than the count of eight; ten and ye are out, my good lad, and out's out and ye be one scrapper of a boyo.

Aware of her movement behind him, he saw from a prickly corner of his mind's eye his long-dead father, right index finger rubbing left side of upper lip as if combing it down, and saying, chorus-like: "Take no notice, son, take no notice. Sufficient unto the day the evil thereof."

Diarmuid came fully awake, found himself alone on his lookout point, the alien foam breathing there before him. He walked back, as if a young man in his determined and rapid head-down stride, fetched the battered binocs from above the dresser, returned to his favoured spot above the sea, and trained them on the patch, a quarter mile southwest. As usual, he had to adjust the left lens before he could gain focus. Gremlins my foot, bloody kids up to nothing but tomfoolery. Useless, plain useless.

There, the middle rose and fell oddly, languidly, twelve to fifteen inches above the gently breathing sea. He saw a curtain of tide coming in with its gift.

"Now what the be-jeeps?" He decided to give Anne-Marie's garden weeds another afternoon of reckless freedom – the kind in which he stoutly believed – and sallied forth to investigate, grabbing a pair of oars and spurs from the shed. "Damn tourists, eat their picnics in my boat, they do, they do. Can't trust nobody," and he added, chuckling as he rubbed his eyes, "not even me. I'm a gas man, I am."

Five minutes later he leaned over a bollard, around the base of which lay his chain, padlocked. The swollen top of the bollard prevented his loop from being lifted off by idle curious and Cork city marauders alike. Bloody hooligans. The chain stretched ten feet out over the harbour, there tied to his stern line, the new blue rope not yet stained by algae. Too much taut tension from the boat and bow anchor for any eejit to pull the chain in, undo the knot, help themselves to my punt, thank you very much. One day I'll catch the buggers who fling stones at it, I will, wait and see I will. Upside down with 'em and over the edge, a boot up the backside, that'd learn 'em quick as petrol fire. Real medicine, none of yer mollycoddlin' modern muck.

He saw a contradiction, remembered the swish of a certain soutane, growled, "Some people don't know no don't, others don't know nothing but."

He fitted the key, ready for the increase in tension, and, with the released mooring line, pulled his red-gunwaled punt in toward the stone steps. He leapt aboard, fitted the spurs, began bailing, one motion. The bilge water smelled vaguely of mackerel, pollack, eel, sandy-bottomed dogfish. Next year, like eleven years ago – the past a terrier with a bone, ye can't no way shake free of it, and why should ye? – why I'll pry out the dried oakum and do a thorough job re-caulking, I will. Stop. The smell of oakum, the feel, the pounding in. Time for a new gunwale too, almost now – brother Ciarán – better dead than red, but no matter, if ye get my fecking meaning. Jabber jabber. Paint the town red too. And God He my hair. God's politics politics for all that.

Securing the bow line, one end permanently attached to his buoy, to the hole in Rufous' Rock so that he could re-moor easily, he pushed off with memories of how knacky his father'd been with ropes. Now, he grinned, let's put the priest to proper use. He took a sightline from the priest's chimney to the patch; then sighted a corner of a field, filled with flowering ragwort, well past the chimney that would keep him straight: keep me in line, a wife of a corner of a field, steady as she goes is old Anne-Marie, thigh or no thigh.

Back into the oars, sore back, back into harness, long harness. He realised he felt good rowing. This who I am. He valued it, as if it were a friend: ye know right where ye be with it, no mystery; ye can count on it to do exactly what ye want it to do. No moodiness in an oar, by God. Yes, but what surprise either? Still, I could've been born with an oar in me hand. Better than a silver spoon in me mouth. An oar for a sceptre. If kings had calluses wouldn't the world be better steered! Tell that one in the pub tonight. To the right person. The wrong. Who cares. To God. Gas man.

He feathered the oars even though there wasn't a puff of breeze, establishing rhythm, and it wasn't but ten strokes before he felt he'd always been rowing. Forever and ever. Non-stop, my man. He was losing himself in a sense of rhythm, yes, but damn Anne-Marie's rhythm, each stroke, or lack of stroke, a nail driven home. Coffin. Fetters and freedom. The point, not just to finish, to lay ahem the slates, to have the roof watertight, to conceive boom diddle-oh, but to climb inside each whack of the hammer, to listen to the sound as it goes up the scale, the nail first long and deep, short and shrill, in and home, next please. Oh bollocks but for a family of fifteen, not this modern conservative everything-in-its-right-place bit, damn the rhythm method, but sprawling, neat when necessary, say on Sunday, but unkempt and spontaneous too, just to live now and then in an all-of-a-sudden way, like now, like off again God knows where, the devil. And give the old boy his due. Under the oxters too.

He twisted to check his progress. A hundred yards to go. One end of the patch looked considerably narrower than the other, the whole thirty-two, thirty-four feet long. Maybe, just maybe, the little boy in the middle-aged man whispered, I'm approaching some treasure, some mystery floating in on the tide. But he knew. He could still think it, but he knew. Thought don't have to have boundaries, like relationships, like farms, this mine, that yours, you may go no further, halt. Danger: Bull. He imagined a new sign at the foot of his harbour-side farm drive: "Warning: Proceed at your own delight."

A putrid smell reached him well before he the carcass. Whale or basking shark he couldn't determine, so rotted was the almost amorphous mass. He could tell which the head, which the tail, little else. The flesh, pitted, had a hard rubbery texture, some twisted white strips dangling down like kelp. Conjuring up miles of intestines, he rowed around and around the corpse, occasionally poking the mass with an oar blade. He laughed and said aloud, "If that porridge don't put hair on your chest, it'll take it off. Fit for a fucking king. Fit for someone what says don't."

He discerned a two-foot-long fin at the base of the head, noted that the tail spread evenly apart, some five feet, that the dorsal fin had all but disappeared, that a small eye, like a pig's, looked mournfully blank.

Then the thought struck him, making him grin: if he could secure the putrid, decomposing hulk in a little cove, he could cut him up, salvage the bones. Wouldn't they, weather-blanched on the garden wall, attract the B&B crowd into the house? Maybe sister Moira could even sell some in her craft shop, "Whale ribs for sale. Special once-off offer. £19.95." How many ribs in a whale? And was the female made from one too? Yes, maybe them bones would rise again, pay for a kicker for the boat, fifteen hundred quid worth. He saw his fanciful thoughts, like the weeds in the garden, spread out and run riot. He knew it, and could hear, as if on the muted sound system in the Skibbereen funeral parlour where he'd been for Aunt Mary's memorial service, his father's quiet refrain, "Take no notice."

He slowly returned to the pier, to the bollard, to home, sat on his lookout point beside the garden, pondered.

Anne-Marie brought him a plate of sandwiches, a mug of coffee, said awkwardly, "I hope you're not planning on more mackerel, Diarmuid. The freezer's full, over-full."

All he answered was, "No girl, no, no, no, not today girl," and keep looking off into the middle distance.

She hesitated, finally couldn't ask him again about the garden, her garden, with his help, for she'd no back, not since Roisín, their second daughter. He in one of his mulling moods, she knew better than to provoke. "Marriage be better than no marriage," her mother had counseled her over the years, but hadn't mentioned what Anne-Marie had come to call "them dead-end days." What, after all, did he give her? Hangovers?

He seemed, she thought, looking back, part animal. He can sit there for hours, alert as a feral cat in first light in a field, crouching statue-still but brimming with pounce for mouse or vole. He do nothin' and then everything bang. Work, or drink, or suss out. She returned to the laundry. Or me.

He didn't turn but could visualise her walking off, the way her head bent slightly to the left, the way her right foot turned in the last six inches of each of its thrusts forward. But he noticed that he could not see what he wanted to see.

So he looked out, trained what he called his crow's eye – his left eye had a clarity his right lacked, at least at distances – on the leviathan's tidal movements; he corrected, his leviathan's movements.

The next day he watched a lobster fisherman who normally berthed beside the pier in the other island harbour motor in to the corpse, for it still lolled about in roughly the same area, just a bit nearer the far foreshore. But Pádraig soon moseyed off about his business, certainly not about His Father's, thought Diarmuid, who remembered a story of how Pádraig had used a grant to buy his boat for the sake of "educational tourism". The only thing he'd ever educated was a conger eel when he broke its back for having stole into one of his pots. And no harm in that, no, not in neither.

Biding his time, Diarmuid waited until Pádraig, as was his wont, clambered up onto the pier where he stored his second string of twenty-five pots. He asked all the usual, until finally, with all the inconsequentiality he could muster, he wondered if Pádraig might give him a hand towing "the visitor" – Diarmuid pointed – to a nearby secluded beach where they could cut him up, mince meat. His neighbour looked strangely at him, grinned, suggested he hop in and they reconnoitre. Diarmuid told him his ideas. Pádraig looked him over again, carefully said not a word.

Once more thick in the stench, it wasn't long before Pádraig made it clear that he'd help tow the whale – for whale he was sure it was, "too big to be one of them bovine basking sharks, and bony besides, and the skin not sandpaper" – but wanted "nothing else whatsoever full-stop to do with the glop." They tied a weight to a piece of rope, tossed it over the tail, fished it out on the other side, made a loop, pulled it tight around the base of the tail. Then they started towing the beast, the engine working hard, exhaust fumes engulfing the men, the massive long-dead weight behind dragging what Diarmuid called its nonexistent heels. Gas man.

He pointed to a sandy cove and they pulled the wreck in as far as they could, then nudged it further into the shallows with the bow. Diarmuid hopped out, adeptly secured the tow rope to a boulder. If the rope held, the whale – please God no shark – would stay put and at low tide, he reckoned, at his leisure, he could cut off the flesh, separate the bones. Sell 'em, make a week's wage for a day's work.

The next morning, while putting two pounds of diesel in his car – more would bring the level up to that tiny hole in the tank that leaked going up the steep hills – Diarmuid chatted with old Johnny, cap down over forehead, who recalled that some eighteen years ago, when a whale washed in, several uncles and he had cut up the tons of flesh with bread knives and collected vertebrae, still relics about the island, some bones west of the Bird Obs, others beside the Master's gate.

Half an hour later Diarmuid set forth, armed with Anne-Marie's bread knife, and, waist deep in stained water, began making incisions. After three hour's surgery about the head, and succeeding in nothing except covering himself in a viscid noisome grease, he had to call it a day, the tide now in. But I'll show the bugger who's who. The winter waves'll do my work for me.

He returned home, dripping, sauntered with a touch of hangdog excitement into the kitchen to have his tea, and finally to tell Anne-Marie what he was about. She sniffed him before she saw him, ordered him out out out, not in her kitchen, how could he, honestly, after all, in God's name, holy suffering Jesus.

"No buts," she said. "None. The health inspector'd close us down,

Diarmuid. Like that." She snapped her fingers. "The immersion's been on all morning. Don't touch nothin' except the inside of the tub. And throw your clothes out the window. Jesus, Mary and Joseph, Diarmuid. You're nothing but a child, a little spoilt child."

"Sometimes I wish I was. I'd get more attention at night."

"You get all the attention you deserve so."

"Ye and your priest."

"You're not to come between me and our God."

"Why not? He's come between ye and me. And he's not 'our' God. He's yours. And ye can have 'im, lock, stock, and barrel."

"We've been through this before, Diarmuid. Be a man, not an animal."

"Get off your pedestal."

"If I'm on one, ye put me there."

"I've put ye nowhere, Anne-Marie. It's ye've put me somewhere, in a freaking limbo."

"We have sex when it's safe, and that's when I'm in a woman's way, and that's that. Period."

"And when is that period, tell me, dear major of a wife."

"When the good Lord sees fits, and not before. Please Diarmuid," tears catching light, "I won't be sinning just to make you feel good for a few bloody seconds."

"I won't be sinning just to make you feel good," he repeated in a hiss as he stalked off. He left the kitchen door, normally closed because of the B&B guests, open. Anne-Marie, weeping, slammed it, then stood in the centre of the kitchen, hands flat on the table, and stared at the oven door. Feeling her heart crossways, she crossed herself and glanced toward the ceiling.

Diarmuid, stalking straight to the rear of the house, and finally leaning against the outside of the windowless east gable, heard his father's voice once more: "Three things, my son, we'll never understand: The ebb and flow of the tide, the work of the honey bee, and the movement of a woman's mind, which surpasses the speed of light."

Two nights later, by chance, if chance there be – he wondered – he met the temporary island nurse in the pub and fell to talking, number six. He learned he'd run serious risk. "Had ye had an open cut on ye," she said sternly, "ye might have contracted septicemia. Ye never know what infections live in long-dead flesh, Diarmuid. Some treasure that would've been, eh?"

He shook it off. "Infections me arse. What else can ye do when your hand's already in the mouth of the dog?"

And then, number seven, he heard from another fisherman neighbour that that dead whale had been on the shipping news two weeks ago, an object fifteen meters long floating about the Fastnet. To be avoided and posing a serious risk to local fishing boats.

His friend-in-arms, he knew. The bouquet was right. Number eight. Maybe if Anne-Marie wore such perfume, he joked with himself, I'd have no difficulty. That'd teach me better than any parish priest. Island man. Gas man. For three spaces of time.

The next night, no sooner had he ordered number two, than he was pulled aside by the manager of the campsite and discreetly informed, in the corner by the stairs, that that whale high and dry in the cuas at low tide was beginning to reek so badly that his campers three hundred yards downwind were complaining.

"You put him there, you move him, Diarmuid. You're a master at pullin' the very devil by the tail. You and him, thick as a cow and a cock of hay."

"I'm after waiting for my friend to rot so's I'll have his bones."

"And when'll that be, you chancer?"

"A month, two."

"I won't have a campsite by then. I'll have a cemetery. And no one there save the spirit of your brilliant find."

"The wind'll change."

"And it'll change again, and again. But the stink won't change. You know, Diarmuid, it'd be a shame to have to take legal action. But if my campers start leaving because" – and here he poked Diarmuid in the chest with his stubby forefinger – "of your effing whale, I'm going to court, hell or high water. That's the cut of my tide, friend."

Diarmuid investigated at midnight, number eight or no number eight. The manager, blast his knobbly balls, he was bleeding right. Dead right, the crotchety bugger. Not only did a stench fill the air, but, in the light of his torch, a gauzy grey petroleum slick appeared to be covering as much of the inner harbour as his light could reach. Blubber? Oil? he wondered. That tail in the same plane as the dorsal fin could well be twisted ninety degrees, don't you know, high-de-ho. Has to be flukes.

But then again, he'd heard stories of how his ancestors on Cape used to burn basking shark oil in their lamps. Aunt Marie sworn by it, said electricity, when it arrived in '72, weren't nothin' but the work of the devil, the same devil that'd blown off her roof when lightning struck. That was in '57. Now wouldn't that have been some sight? How she'd trembled, flesh on a stick, whenever she heard thunder thereafter, poor thing. What a bang that must've been. God's crack. Craic. Gas man. God's a gas man. That's the real goat's toe, me boy.

The next morning, high tide, he rowed over to the cuas, unloosed the rope, bits of flesh hanging from it. Pádraig's boat no where to be seen, he struggled to pull his whale out to open sea with his punt. After a half hour of putting his back into it, he'd no sense of any rhythm, no Anne-Marie rhythm, no rowing rhythm, no anything rhythm, for fuck's sake. He could feel back and shoulder muscles knotting either side of his neck. Like pulling a locomotive with your bare hands, and off the track, and through the ditches.

Three hundred yards gained, sweat pouring down him, making his thwart slippery, he heard an outboard approaching: a yachtsman in his flimsy dinghy had taken pity and come along side, his son with hand pinching nose. They took over the rope. With their two-and-a-half horse kicker, they slowly succeeded in dragging the whale another three hundred yards, now back to the mouth of the inner harbour where Diarmuid had first spotted him. And there, at Diarmuid's gesture, they let him go, the tide having started to ebb.

Good-bye law suit, good-bye treasure; 'tis an ill whale that brings no man any good. He thanked father and son, suggesting lamely that despite the smell "ye've had an adventure ye'd never have had before, no, nor certainly would never have again, no, no, no. May ye live to be as old as Methuselah's cat!" Looking at each other, with perhaps something else in mind, they nodded.

For the next two weeks he watched his creature. It had floated calmly back into the harbour the next day, had gotten stuck inside a far cave. Let the manager do something about that, let him sue God for all he's worth. Should he stay there, he'll rot – and then I'll claim the sunken bones, fish 'em up with me grappling iron. And should he wash out on the tide, and the change of wind, so be it. Take no notice, my son.

That thought, he tackled the garden. In one day had it weeded. On the next he started breaking ground for the new shed he'd promised

Anne-Marie. He'd have the slates on before gale season started, he would, of that she could be sure.

And sure but I'll give her a bottle of stinky perfume for Christmas – just to remind me of certain god-forsaken boundaries. And don't try to sneak off, thigh. Be part of my treasure. Beach me, Anne-Marie, number one. I'm your whale, ye of the thigh-bone mine. Number two. Gas man? Me? Now who, dear brother, ain't?

Temper, Temper

Sits there, fuming, computer screen in a wink a storm of grains. The last hour of adding and re-adding the slippery budget totals for the year of Our Lord Nineteen Hundred and Ninety-Nine, gone in an electronic twinkling. "Office Supplies", "Estimated Income from Sponsors", "Business Trips", "Miscellaneous", all the figures re-juggled in the light of the last hectic three weeks, all, he fears, down the bleeding drain. An hour's work, glug glug glug. He growls, gathers phlegm, hawks a gob into the scrap basket.

As if on cue, the lights go off, the monitor dies.

Screams obscenities, sits in semi-darkness, stunned by events, disgusted by self.

In the ensuing silence, he hears wife gather up project, hears door to conservatory click shut, knows his tantrum has evicted her. Hears something else, gusts rattling slates.

"What the bejesus?" Jumps from desk, storms about study, stares out the east gable's single pane. Listens. Can't concentrate. Begins pacing, sweeps downstairs, through the conservatory, into the extension, up creaky stairs to bedroom. No wife.

Out leaky windows, eyes the sullen sea, spots spray rising from furthest headland. Focuses on the near, the escallonia, the old apple trees, tossing about the garden borders. "No poem today, pal. Let alone those fecking figures."

He curses as he walks involuntarily about the house, comes again to look out bedroom windows at sea spray sweeping across the island, the very air thick with rising storm, the sea emitting tell-tale greasy glint. From around the corner an outdoor chair sails into the walled herb garden. The barbecue stand vanishes into the euonymous. The chimney cowling of the neighbouring house disappears and, as if in sympathy, his house begins to fill with puffs of acrid smoke. Feels twinge of curiosity mix with anger.

Lights flicker, cut out two seconds later. He taps barometer, which drops from the 'S' of "Stormy" to the bottom of the bowl, a forty-five degree fall. Yes, he decides, the wind, she's calling. Fu-dge fig-ures.

Returns to study, shuts off all the dead equipment, hustles downstairs, unplugs hi-fi, washing machine, fax, returns to bedroom. Purple sprouting broccoli withers before his eyes. He wanders into conservatory, sees it's already caked with salt, a month's deposit in fifteen minutes.

Bumps into wife. All the time in bathroom. She looks hard at him, shakes her head. "Sorry," he says, points at his head with index finger, taps skull, nods.

They sally forth, agreed that what to do but witness humdinger of intensifying storm.

Even as they struggle to make it to their banger, gusts strike like punches. Deirdre staggers off-course twice into garden, Harry onto compost heap. Gaining drive and bracing himself behind van door so that he can hold it open for her, he wonders if a little outing hasn't already become too much of an ordeal.

Down the steep dirt road. Stopping every fifty yards to observe waves crashing against cliffs and billowing over massive areas where they'd never before seen sea.

Decide they'd better lay in an extra supply of such basics as milk. With no ferry scheduled for Christmas anyway, who knows how long ferryless.

Descending to North Harbour, they notice the ferry's out, learn it made the nine o'clock run to Baltimore, leaving before the winds were in earnest. They wonder whether it will, or is, chancing a return.

Enter Siopa Beag. As they wait in line, sipping hot whiskeys and eating a pile of waffles cordially offered by Emer and Michael, the wind ups the ante. The metal roof roars. And they're in darkness, the electricity off over the entire island, not just their townland.

They learn the ferry left Baltimore at 11:15. It's now noon, a little after.

As if pulled by a force they don't understand, they batter their way through the gusts to a breakwater that affords a view of Roaringwater Bay. No ferry in sight. Others join them. They realise they're all here because they're frightened, frightened of the storm, frightened for the safety of the boat, those aboard. Stories of sea tragedies fill their heads. They sense generations of past islanders staring out to sea, waiting, praying. There's no banter, no gossip, just a small crowd of grim faces trying to discern the ferry, hoping it into ken.

At 12:30 they glimpse her. The crowd gasps as a breaking swell hides her from sight for longer than they think possible. Harry hears a seaman say "there's no badness in the seas yet", but he wonders. A loose drawstring tip stings Harry's cheek. He tucks it in, conscious it could injure eye. Checks out North Harbour, notices that despite its sheltered position it's all white horses. A sheet of spray lifts off its surface. He imagines the whitecaps whipped by some angry god and doesn't wonder why wild times bring out pagan imaginings.

The *Naomh Ciarán*, as if in slow motion, makes her approach, despite her frequent disappearing acts, toward the harbour mouth. When she's past the stacks he knows she's "in" in the nick of time.

As she draws near the pier, seven men stand ready to secure hawsers to bollards off stem and stern. Around 20 mightily relieved Islanders watch. A few are crying, relieved to see their loved ones safely home. After the half-dozen passengers disembark, including the visiting priest, there to celebrate Christmas Eve Mass, the ferry lads set out to move the ship from outer to safe harbour.

As soon as the ferry's loosed from her fair-weather berth, she's blasted by such invisible ferocity that in seconds she's pinned against the adjacent pier, the Bull's Nose. The team of men ashore huddle at the ready. When a lull comes and the skipper's orders given, they move with dispatch, tugging the heavy hawsers from bollard to bollard, sometimes hand-winching them. They keep bow and stern secured even while the twin engines rev; otherwise the screaming wind will swing the hull about and the boat herself become a loose cannon on the harbour's pitching deck.

When the final bollards are looped, everyone relaxes, breathes the big breaths of conscious relief. Shoulders drop. It took the ferry an hour plus to steam the 8 miles "in" to Cape, another half-an-hour to move the final 100 yards.

Deirdre and Harry head for home, park, check roof, windows, run for the lee of indoors.

Still down is the computer, which Harry usually says looks after him, and shortly the water supply peters out, so down goes the rest of the kitchen, which similarly looks after Deirdre. They know better than to open fridge or freezer doors, or to flush the john, except in an emergency. "Irony of irony," Harry announces, "this Christmas, time to conserve rather than to give."

Deirdre wants to walk a cake to a neighbour. Tries three times in the next two hours to navigate the drive but, as soon as she leaves the garden gate and turns west, out of the shelterbelt, the wind blocks her way. Once she's thrown backwards against the rear of the van.

Harry sets off to try to photograph the storm. Bundled up, wearing snorkeling mask and thick leather ski gloves, he works his zigzag way down to An Oige. Every few steps he's bustled off route into pasture. Twice he's flattened. To his surprise, he's delighted, feels himself in an adventure rather than a pickle or – he can't not remember – a tantrum.

Ducking behind the Old Telegraph House, he snaps pictures of thick sea spray hurling through the air over the roof of the hostel. When he raises his goggles to set the camera accurately, raindrops sting like nastily thrown pebbles. Hunkering behind a seawall, he attempts to capture the waves breaking against the pier and feels he's on the front line in some mythic war. Howling furies attack across the harbour. He hears heavy artillery pounding. The roof behind him's already holed.

In front of the priest's house, sheltering behind the garage, he shoots 10 frames. Taking in the turmoil, he stands aghast as Fineen's punt rises like a giant kite into the air, flips around, twisting and turning, flies out of the hostel yard, over the stone wall, and from 20 feet up nose-dives into the road in front of the slipway, somersaults, comes to rest against the priest's wall, hull split open. Only then does he remember his camera – and that two minutes earlier he was walking where the rowboat crash-landed. From an odd corner of his mind he sees he's too exited to lose his temper.

He makes his way to Ballyieragh, the townland west of the harbour. Easier to walk here because of protection from the hills. Removes goggles. Gawks. The waves crashing against the point blow his mind. He slowly realises he's experiencing waves as though they're miracles, gifts from another world. The elements aren't now at war, he concludes, but at cosmic play. Places where he's been serenely perched in what he previously reckoned severe storms have waves blasting over them, places 70 feet straight up from the sea. It finally dawns on him: "Hey, this here's hurricane."

At South Harbour's three-fifths-of-a-mile-wide mouth, mammoth waves stretch half the distance between Blanan and the Bullig, the opposing points. When these marauding immensities smash against land, thick whiteness exploding halfway up 300-foot cliffs, Harry hears a chthonic booming not unlike thunder, wonders if this is how gods chuckle.

Looks at the troubled sky, at his watch, and, while he doesn't wish to leave this scene – of destruction and creation both – he also doesn't dare risk the mile hike home in darkness. If something's coming at him, slate or boat or rogue wave, he wants a chance at evasive action.

Home safe sound and full of nature, Deirdre too, her cake delivery accomplished during a brief lull, telephone still working, they discover, house lit by twelve candles, that it's relaxing, utterly relaxing, a complete change of pace: can't read, can't watch TV, can't listen to music, can't surf the Net. Can't be, as he remembers T. S. Eliot writing of modern man, "distracted from distraction by distraction." They sit before the smoky fire, savor the stormy peace, rub each other's feet.

He recognises he's somehow given up his prized possession, will power. Not trying to do anything. Not trying to fix the computer, recalculate his figures, take a photo, prove himself. "Hey," he sighs. Deirdre hears the happiness.

They drive to nine o'clock Mass. The one-lane main road's full of parked cars, the Church cold but strangely pure. And such candlelight: candles in every window, candles spread about on the altar rail, on the altar itself. When Father Cadogan opens the service, he flicks on not the mike but a faint hand-held torch and shines it on his texts. The wind roars, subsides into a long moan, roars afresh. Father Cadogan reminds the congregation that rough circumstances took Mary and Joseph, too, by surprise – and on this self-same night.

During the three ferryless days following, Harry learns from a fisherman neighbour that gusts in the region reached 140 mph. In "Weather Eye", he reads, meteorologist McWilliams places the storm amongst the five worst of the century.

Computer up and running, photos sufficient unto the day, Harry confesses that, in the aftermath of the Christmas Eve hurricane, he encountered throughout Oileán Chléire – and throughout himself – a renewed sense of what's essential. But, after all, he stresses, smiling, he did set out for basics.

He scans his study. Hanging from the monitor, a present from Deirdre, a sign she drew and decorated, Carlson's Two Commandments: 1, Don't sweat the small stuff. 2, Remember, it's all small stuff. Yeah, he thinks. Maybe even death. Perspective, pal.

With red pen, he draws a heart around the corny reminder, trusts he'll be ready for the next random visit. Anger. Yes, he chuckles inwardly, best leave it to the Lord, at least for the rest of this millennium.

Go-Devil

Andy couldn't see that this thing called 'soul' had anything to do with a buck rake, nor that this half-demented creature named 'Auntie' had anything to do with God. But then, had this power called God anything to do with any of them, let alone with him? And, he wondered, is a buck rake – a part of the universe, albeit one handy man-made contraption – not also a part of His Nibs?

He shook his head, muttering, as he navigated the rust-riddled John Deere down the savagely rutted lane – one of the main roads of the still car-less island. A hooded crow, perched on a fence post beside the lane, took off peremptorily as Andy approached, circled once over head, flew straight for the Napoleonic Watchtower. Andy felt as if he'd just been frisked by a security guard of Kingdom Come.

Intuiting that it had rained hard enough last night so that he ran less risk of spinning a back wheel in the muck if he shifted into four-wheel drive and raised the ten bales of hay he'd secured atop the buck rake with an old anchor rope, he stopped, shifted, throttled down that touch, thought of dismounting from the tractor, genuflecting, then kicking ass.

Whose ass he wasn't certain. It wouldn't do to kick Auntie's, as she was, after all, a woman, his father's sister, and in her sixties. But no one else came to mind. Why didn't they get along better, she cooking for him, keeping his house, he, all twenty-two years of him, earning the minimal money to take care of them both? Just this morning, as he was finishing off the fry she'd puttered over as if it were an oil painting, she'd let him have it: "You, Andy, boyo, why be ye so scanty when it comes to getting me to Church of a Sunday? Couldn't you, well, seat me in a cart, have old Jimmy of Thirteen Hands pull us there so? Hey?"

"And why won't you just sit on the top of my tractor wheel-well and let me drive you there. Patrick of the Glen takes his mam that way," he'd answered.

"That's no place for a woman of any age, let alone mine, sonny."

"It works."

"It works for those who like to have their skirts lifted."

"You said that, Auntie."

"And it's time you did something about it."

"About those women?"

"About getting me to Church."

"Auntie, why don't you get over your arthritis and walk. Rub in the poitín Mikey gave you for your birthday. Twice a day, he recommended."

"If I weren't afflicted by arthritis, my buachaill, we wouldn't be having this conversation."

"It's not a conversation."

"Do something, you cág. Other than rub it in. Which doesn't work. I've tried. For two months."

"You do something."

"I do the work inside, you the work outside. You get me to Church, nephew mine. I can't miss another Sunday Mass. 'Twould be a sin. You know, that phenomenon you don't seem to believe in: sin, that which cuts you off from God."

It was then that Andy stomped out of the house, went straight to the John Deere, drove it from beside the calf house to the wide barn doors, and loaded seven bales of hay onto the buck rake, two across, three lengthwise on top of them, two more across. Then he threw an anchor rope around, just in case. Once onto the metal seat, engine running, he pulled the lever that lifted the buck rake – which his Grandda used to call a go-devil – tilted it slightly so that, when going up to the pasture where the cattle grazed on the browned end of winter grass, the bales would still be leaning backwards, toward him, jutting out at the rear of his tractor.

And here he was driving through the muck re-living his morning exchange with his aunt, all he had left of his family, his four sisters married and off the island, his brother in the army, his parents killed in a car crash on the mainland two years back. And then this aunt. God Almighty but she was one stubborn, prim, princess of a woman, what he imagined his Irish teacher would have laughingly labelled a perfect smugachán. No wonder she'd never married, no wonder –

On the pedestrian path known as the Mass Track, or An Cnoicín, coming over the hill from the Church, who should Andy see wending his way through the stubborn intruding brambles and gorse and about to start negotiating the mud just ahead of him but the resident Irish priest, black shoes still somehow shiny. Andy applied the two brake pedals so that there'd be no splash, waited for the priest to walk by. But Father Matt stopped beside him, looked up, shouted above the engine noise, "And where were you today, my son. I've missed you and your aunt these last months. Is anything the matter, with you . . . or with me?"

"Good afternoon, Father Matt." Noting that the priest had planted his feet wide apart, Andy politely switched off the somewhat vociferous engine. "No no, nothing's the matter, it's just that Auntie Josephine's so crippled with her arthritis that she can no longer walk further than around the house," he paused, then added, believing that the priest would recognise and keep a confidence – "and she's so proud she won't be seen atop my tractor wheel well. What else can I do?"

"My son, as no doubt you've heard, I'm a bit of an iconoclast. I've a way of not always going along with what has unfortunately become rigid Church tradition, and I won't be serving here on peaceful Cape much longer. Off to Sierra Leone, I am, in a month's time. May twenty-third of the Year of Our Lord Nineteen Hundred and Sixty-eight. So please tell your aunt that I've missed her, but she's in no danger of losing her soul if she doesn't come to Church to pray and take Communion. God's not out there," he said, gesticulating in a wide circle, "but, for example," – he smiled broadly while thumping his thin chest – "in here, in each and every one of us. Tell your Aunt Josephine that the only way she's likely to lose her soul is by worshipping a god outside herself. He or She or It is everywhere, not just in our Church. Not outside, but inside. We are in God and God is in us. Please assure her of that. And it's implications. And I'll see if I can drop by the house and have a talk with her before I depart, all but excommunicated, for the dark heart of Africa. So, a good day to you, my son."

"And to you, father, and thanks for sharing your whatchamacallit, that iconoclapum," answered Andy, uncertain as to what he had just been told, but determined he'd somehow get to Church next Sunday.

"I-con-o-clas-um. Adjectival form, I-con-o-clas-tic."

"Iconoclasm. Iconoclastic."

"You've got it."

Cogitating, Andy waited a minute as the priest walked away, switched on the engine, motored up to Gort Mor, the pasture with the three feeder rings inside, and lowered the buck rake. Since there was no gate on the lane side, he simply tossed the seven bales over the drystone wall, an act that always brought his herd of twenty-three Guernseys running. He then went over the stile, hauling the bales, one by one – despite the pushing noses – to the feeders. Once there he yanked off the blue twine, gave the bales a quick shake, returned to his tractor for the jug of molasses, retraced his steps to the feeders and poured thick black syrup over the hay, checked the appearance of each cow, scratched a few heads between the ears, uttered a name and a greeting for every cow he touched, returned again to the tractor and drove on up to Paddy Johnny Mike's lay-by, swivelled around by stepping on the right wheel brake while allowing the left wheel to do the work, and headed home.

Why, he pondered, if what Father Matt said was true, then God is in a buck rake, is in me. He – or She or It – isn't just out there, but in here. It's a sin to think otherwise. It's a sin. It's a sin. Maybe it's a sin to think there's sin. Yeah, with the buck rake holy, now I've an iconoclastic clue of how to put it to use.

And here the idea he'd been waiting for, praying for, came to him. If he was going to find him a girl, a colleen he could love, first he'd better lower the voltage in Auntie Jo. Yes, yes, yes: Put that old family sofa on the buck rake, let Auntie Josephine more than perch on the go-devil while I drive her to Church – of a sunny Sunday. She won't be seen on no tractor, no, but on a sofa, yes, yes, that'll do nicely. Thank you, Father Matt. Maybe your beliefs are getting you side-lined or ostracised to Sierra Leone, but yes, thank you, God's in the sofa too. Yes, take God off the pedestal, and the Pope and all those finger-wagging power-prizing priests with Him. Get down into the earth, youngster. Be a worm. Squirm.

Auntie Josephine, ready or not, here I come.

A week later, at ten-thirty in the morning, Andy had all prepared, the buck rake and tractor painted, a new second-hand silencer installed. He invited his aunt to come outside, sit down on the cleaned old parlour ottoman which had been in the barn since his parents' joint wake, and try everything out before the fifteen minute slow careful ride to the Church.

"Sit there, Auntie Jo," Andy pointed. "After I start the engine, I'll lift the buck rake, the sofa'll tilt back just that little bit, and you'll be seated squarely in a queenly throne. Here, let's tuck this blanket around your legs, and then there's no fear of anything being lifted by the wind, your skirt or rumours of any sort. How's that?" he asked as he checked the ropes that made certain no bump could dislodge the sofa.

Auntie Josephine leaned back, folded her arms, said nervously, "Drive out to the lane, stop, check with me. We'll see if we proceed with this system or if you take me back home."

They were off. A minute later, at the foot of the drive, Andy shifted into neutral, put on the emergency brake, and climbed off to check, his heart racing, he imagining God sitting on a go-devil.

Auntie Jo peered down at him, said simply, "You've rigged this sofa absolutely snasta, my lad. I think I've been waiting for this way to Church all my adult life."

"Onward it is, Auntie Jo?"

"Onward, Andy. And thank you. From this height I feel as though I'm seeing the island for the very first time. I'm almost flying, slow motion flying. I can see over hedgerows, over the drystone ditches. And I've never seen over them before. No wonder Father Matt was talking to me about changing perspectives yesterday when he dropped by. My dear, God's in everything, even your handy work."

As they travelled the rough island mile, they met no other traffic, as there weren't yet any cars on the island, nor any tarred roads, but some hundred and eighty persons were making their way to Church from a variety of directions. And when each and every one saw Josephine sitting on the sofa, she herself some six feet up in the air, the ends of the sofa only a foot or so away from the drystone ditches either side, and she looking more like Queen Elizabeth than one of the O'Driscoll clan, jaws fell slack. No one pointed, no one laughed, and many thought of bowing. A few crossed themselves, though whether they were afraid for her or of her and invoking divine protection wasn't clear. Still, she didn't seem to notice.

And, as he lowered the buck rake in front of the Church gate so that Auntie Josephine could stand up, with a helping hand from him, Andy felt that this thing called 'sofa' had something to do with God in a buck rake, and that this creature named 'Auntie' had similar family connections. Grinning, he sympathised with those who'd crossed themselves as well. And then, he concluded, if God was inside them all, and in the buck rake etcetera etcetera etcetera, well then, more power, and more humility, and more humus, to us all.

Maybe this coming summer, he fantasised, when all the girls'll be here for the Irish College, and their young teachers too, maybe His Nibs might point one out. If I make the effort. Why, that hill over there, the highest on the island, that could be the mountain of suffering, and those cliffs to the southeast of it, they could be the cliffs of death. But here, right now, this is the tractor of life. Since I've probably only one life to live, at least as far as I know, now's the time to go for it. Auntie Josephine in the go-devil, triggered by Father Matt beside the tractor, have set me free, free as the humus in my compost heap. And God in me but it's time I got down to the business – or play – of living. Yeah, if there is such a thing as sin, that thing of banjax power, it cuts you off not from God but from yourself. What a joke, the normal take on sin. Giddy-up, you horse of a tractor, you carriage of a buck rake, he thought as he climbed back in the seat prior to parking it. Let's see what this priest of iconoclasm has to say today now that my go-devil's arrived.

Giddy-up

Physically, sissy sesquipedalian me's been next-to-nowhere, boarding school, the streets and lanes and culs-de-sac of Cork, all – for the last seventy-two years – tappety tap tap tap. Me with my stick, dog or no dog. But then that nephew Jimmy sends me a walloping five hundred smackeroos for birthday splurge, with challenge attached: "Auntie Aggie please to take a holyday somewhere youse never been and do something youse never done. Blah dee blah dee blah. XXX, your best worst & one & only nephew, Jimmy." The very idea – as Betsy read me the card – gave me the willies. Watch out, you hyperborean Watercourse Road. You clogging arteries and veins.

So I decided to do a razzmatazz. Looked this old creature over. Nothing callipygian here. But thanks to my Dog-scan noticed something missing between the ribs. But couldn't tell what. But. Certainly no absence of flesh thereabouts. Certainly no fingerprints from Adam. But I was, I have to admit, getting shorter-tempered than usual, as quick to peck as Éamon Kelly's unfed hen. I saw that there's no reason nowadays, what with even my computer able to talk (thank God the keyboard's exactly the same as the Perkin's Brailler), that bills from major companies like the ESB and Eircom, couldn't send me the monthly damages in Braille. If old AIB can render monthly statements readable by Braille printouts, why not the other big fellas? Well, over the phone I suddenly found myself reading ESB and Eircom riot acts. I really don't like having Betsy, faithful next-door neighbour Betsy of the loveliest perfumes – perfumes she dashes on her wrists each morning before she glues herself to the window, reports Jimmy, to watch her husband walk away to work – have to enunciate all the fissiparous ins and outs of my personal finance and legerdemain when she so gratuitously goes over the daily post with me.

Well, when Betsy read me Jimmy's card for the third time, and again the amount of the cheque, I hunched there in my front parlour, puzzled, quiet as what I'm told is a decorative standing lamp beside me, the noise of heavy articulated trucks entering spaces in my head as if they'd never been filled before. And as I heard Betsy subtly reinserting card into envelop, I slumped like a skinny statue with tummy in my only easy chair, felt my stick legs straighten out, my stick lower arms – in contradistinction to certain upper – fall off the arm-rests and dangle like the pull-chain in the loo. Jason changed position, licked my knobbly left hand, tossed his woodland odour up at me.

"Well?" Betsy finally dared inject into the silence.

"Well," I answered, taking an audible deep breath as I descended from some ethereal world to the rough-and-tumble uneven-pavement-city publicly proclaimed hereabouts as Earth. "All the way from the Middle East, this letter, this money. Old Jimmy boy. Jimmy Noonan. Here I thought him but a poor peacekeeping soldier stationed in the Lebanon and not some CEO gallivanting about God's ex-kingdom with a slush fund at his disposal. Well, here be it acknowledged that thanks to his suggestion and generosity, his humanitarian magnanimity, yes," – I held my breath, relegated myself to the edge, let emotional vertigo tug my apron strings – "I'm going to dive off the deep end of Fisherman's Wharf. Well, maybe I won't go quite as far as six thousand miles. Seventy ought to do the trick. Build a new omphalos when I arrive."

"Do what?" whispered Betsy. "Other than listen to another talking book, I mean."

"Hand me the Irish Guide Dog Association's bimonthly. On the ledge in front of the windows, last I saw it."

By sound and shuffle and fresh whiff of pristine perfume I could discern Betsy'd spotted it on a table by the door. She touched it to my right hand, clearly watched my two Sherlock Holmes fingers scan it from cover to cover. Fifteen minutes later, with not a single peep from Bet, I lifted my right hand high into the air, and grunted, "Found it. My digits may be all but mincemeat, but here 'tis, the advertisement that's set me heart a-pounding. My fate." I breathed a-fresh. Slow. Long. "This magazine my Tao te Ching. There!" I stabbed the approximate spot. "If it weren't for that old Western Road roaring by in front of this excuse for a row house, and you next door rather than here, you'd have heard the thumping of this here suck pump amplified through double-cavity walls – or ribcage."

"What? You okay, Aggie?"

"Just a little ad with a magnet in it and the tips of my fingers filled with iron filings."

"And?"

"It says" – my Sherlocks flew over the next-to-last page, stopped – "'Goat Husbandry Course for Beginners. Taught by experienced Mark Collins on Remote Irish Island. Call 028 919919.' Listen up."

I played the tape that came with the journal, heard Mark himself give a few more enticing details.

"Hand me the phone, gal."

"Now, Aggie. Let's discuss the pros and–"

"The phone please darlin'."

The next day I lifted the receiver on the second ring.

"Ah, 'tis you, Jimmy boy. Yes, I've done it. Yes. Cape Clear Island. Oileán Chléire. Off the south coast, not Galway. No. Now Jimmy, you know me, I've barely been in the countryside and never on a boat. Not into gangplanks any more than art museums. And no, I don't know a pandemic lusty goat from a sterile fusty unicorn. No, I wouldn't want to have to separate sheep from goats regardless. Not a nice occupation. Leave that to the expert. Anyway, yes, I called this Mark and had some talk. No, not my usual palaver, nephew. He asked when I'd like to come. Told him next week! Yes, almost had it over and done with before I started. You know how sometimes you connect with people you've never met, connect better than with someone you've known for fifty years. Well, not so many in your case, buster. No. Yes. Well, I learned he's blind too, not since birth like me, but since age three, and he's nowhere near my age, almost a baby in fact, a mere forty-eight. Haven't I some effrontery to have asked! And look out, such tact might be in your priestly genes too. Anyway, Mark too is getting on nicely in the dark, and he's recommended a B&B cheek by jowl to his place, and we'll do six hours of goat work a day for three days for forty euros a day. With Jodie's B&B forty-two a day, full room and board, and the bus from Cork to Baltimore and the ferry free to OAP's – et al. – with travel passes, not to mention the handicapped, that leaves ample for socialising in island pubs, whatever. And I guess there's a dearth of whatever on Cape. So I'm off on the Monday. Into the wild blue yonder. Mark says he knows some locals who haven't left Cape in over forty years. So I'll be in good company. Yes, my dear, I feel just like a kid. No pun intended. Excited. Scared." Teetering's the word. "God bless, nephew mine."

When I hung up, I sat down in the straight-backed chair beside the phone and, smelling a peat bog, scratched Jason between the ears. No prayer arch in my back – or in his. Aloud I said, "Goats, me dear." I ran my hand down his back, aware of tiny hard bumps. Over and over I petted them. When an air-borne hair touched the base of my nostrils, I remembered he was in shedding mode. "Well, counsellor," I said at last, "Cape Clear Island to learn about goats. Whatcha think?" And Jason, at least as he exists in my imagination, promptly replied, "Right on!" (By such Americanisms you can tell he curls beside me late at night while I fall asleep listening to Grisham reading Grisham.)

'Twas then I perforce really started to think about goats, not as metaphor for the unknown, nor as symbols for certain urges, but as purely warm-blooded, domesticable creatures. What would it be like to run my hands along their spines, that is, if one can even feel their spines? Worried, I called three of my so to speak sight-hindered friends, asked if they knew what a goat was like. "A dog with horns." "A small sheep, you silly." A slender cow." And I was shrinking, those spinal disks thinning. My GP'd recently told me I'd lost 4 inches in the last year. And I didn't even know it! Blind as bat midget on the way! No. Yes.

I need a vacation, not an ambivalence.

I need goats, not vertigo.

I need an island. An island's island.

Not an ontological argument but a new omphalos.

And by Zeus them Greeks. Everywhere they went – and they'd plenty of Jimmy in them – they erected an omphalos; everywhere they went became the centre of their down-to-earth world. Not just Mt. Olympus, not just Delphi, Aggie: everywhere.

Riding the bus from Cork's mad main bus station beside the loveless stench of the Lee I found no different from riding the bus from the stop from UCC to Grand Parade, 'cept longer (unless it's a Friday afternoon). But then, Lordy be, on the way to Skibbereen, why, that bus had no suspension system, my stomach and I can tell you. I gave thanks I'd no false teeth, for I knew as well as I know my cranky digits I would've lost 'em after any one of a number of them bumpity bumps. And Jason, who's my retriever and knows how to bring me back from the brink, he's taking a break with Bet.

In Skib I waited to change buses. And waited. And waited. It arrived twenty minutes late, at 1:50 rather than the 1:30 I was told, with the ferry departing Baltimore at 2:15. So I climbed aboard the strangest of all buses ever known to man (read capital W, capital O, man), the Baltimore Special – and then it sashayed as it sped along the road – except when the kindliest, most helpful of drivers had to stop to deliver something to a friend. Twice. Two needy people en route. Would the ferry wait?

That twisting excuse of a road! I could tell by the feel and the sounds that our driver had to stop and back up four times to let vehicles from the other direction by. When loquacious me queried my seat-mate about what was happening, and about the quality of the labyrinthine lanes, he replied, "Missus, if we had them kind of roads down here you have around Cork city and Dublin, without these potholes, and wide as ten horses end to end, why we'd have half the country down here every weekend, and where'd be our peace and quiet then?"

Jouncing along, hearing the side of the road ricochet our own sound back at us as we weaved forward, I found myself reflecting on my nephew, my true world traveller, he who climbed the mountain of Ararat and all but found the ark on the sixteenth day of the six month. O Lord, to have a bus jam my heart crossways.

And then, from the south, I could hear Cape calling. Soon, Aggie, soon. I was reminded of a story about when there weren't any roads and you had to stop your journey wherever you were come night (not – I could feel myself grinning, wrinkle by dry wrinkle – that that would have affected me much). Then you had all the time in the wide wicked world to chew the fat with your companions – or with yourself. But now that we've got these cars and trains and lorries, these buses, and these roads every which way – how far Corinth, neighbour? – there's no more peace. And, maybe what's even worse, there's no more time.

Time. Tempus. Tempest. Fugit inreparabile tempus, you rara avis you. And it's twenty after two.

Upon that possibly penultimate (Parish Priest) bit of moralising memory, I felt the bus come to a halt. "End of the line, lads," the driver called out. "The ferry's a-waitin'." As the movement of those around me receded, I grabbed my stick, let it dangle, and by my hands on seat backs moved step by step to the front. The driver assisted me down the steps, passed me and my bag on to an island man he knew who led me down the pier and onto the ship. Pádraig was his name, and he'd had a blind grandmother, knew just how to navigate me with the gentlest of grips on the flop of my upper arm. And I'll be honest with you, lads, that lackadaisical lappet's a mystery to my GP and to me, given the shape of the rest of my appendages.

Shortly the engine started and did that saloon fill with roar. People sitting next to each other yelled to communicate. I found myself inside not a Tower of Babel, but a Saloon of Screech. And I've sat in squeaky rocking chairs, but not chairs that go up and down, and side to side, and back and forth, amid tintinnabulation – and then some. Whoa, I tell ya, I thought I must be cowgirl Doris Day – a Calamity Jane before she became a virgin – in the great wild west riding a slow motion bucking bronco that brooked no reins. I held onto the bench in front of me, that bench back my faithful highfalutin father's pommel. But no agallop for this, a, mare.

When cantankerous me complained to Paddy of the noise, he hollered that it might be quieter if we went outside onto the stern deck. So he guided me most carefully – without my stick – out. Once outside, I couldn't say that the sound was easier on my eardrums. A few decibels maybe, but nothing to write home about. And who's home? Nothing to write Jimmy or Betsy about. Nothing to put a face on a story with. Paddy told one of the crew of my hearing sensitivity, and this gentleman quickly came up with a solution: "Come with me, missus. I'll take you up the steep stairs to the wheelhouse – because inside there – now don't tell anyone – it's the quietest place aboard. You might not hear the clock tick, but a stage whisper fills the cabin."

With my hands on a railing either side of me, and me climbing something very like a ladder, and the ferry pitching and yawing, the crewman, with one hand lightly poised on the curve of my spine, talked me along. He promised he'd catch me if anything went wrong, told me when I'd reached the last step, navigated me into the wheelhouse. I was sat down on a stool beside the skipper and had me a tour of Roaring Water Bay. He shared stories about a rock called Bird Island, and the shipwreck of the Stephen Whitney (out of a hundred and ten, eighteen survivors, all stripped naked by the winds and seas and rocks). He helped me see the Fastnet Lighthouse as if it were some saviour out to sea. Even in the winter, when sometimes he's seen waves break over its lantern. And then I worked up my audacity and asked, "Captain, were you ever scared while standing where you are right now?"

"Only once. Worried many times, scared only once."

"When? No. Why?"

"Well, it was a summer day. Not unlike today. And I looked to the southwest, out toward the Fastnet, and what should I see from there across the sound to the Mizen but a rising line of black. One mammoth black wave rising. I'd never seen such a wave before – and I'm glad to say I've never seen such a wave since. With this ship very ferry full of passengers, I knew I'd no time to reach any harbour. And I worried that if I informed the passengers, they might panic. So I just did what I ordinarily do when a wave of any size approaches: I simply steered straight at it. But this wave, as it drew nearer, it had power unlike any I've ever seen. A tidal wave."

"A tsunami?"

"Exactly. I thought it was curtains, but I kept the ship straight into her. And she was upon us. We rose and rose and rose into the air, I'd say some sixty feet, and I'm not one for exaggeration, and then, you know, she passed under us and down and down and down we went, and that was that. The passengers all had their mouths hanging wide open, and me and the crew too, but it was past. No after effects. Massive surf breaking along the edges of the islands."

"No one hurt?"

"Not around here, ma'am. Not around here. Excuse me now, but we're coming in to Cape's North Harbour, and I've got to concentrate on the landing. But thanks for your company on the way in, and may ye have a fine course with Mark and all his four-legged, bramble-chomping friends."

The patient mate, who never left my side while with the skipper, led me, positioned me, down the ladder-like stairs, me going backward, he below me, ready, the pitching and yawing gone. When the skipper slowed the ferry down some more, the noise disappeared, and my ears felt ready, and rested, and I'd the feeling I was entering a different realm, the very opposite of any Corkonian kingdom come.

Paddy led teetering me off the boat with the same care he'd led me on, took me right up to my B&B lady, shook my hand goodbye. Jodie bustled me into her car, relegating my bag to the boot. And I'd a new world of noise. Her car'd no silencer a-tall. Its roar fit right in with that all around us. She told me that many of the cars and tractors about used a roll-start to get going – a pop-the-clutch trick – so when they parked on the flat pier engines were left a-running. A simple symphony of sound. And as she was backing up on this congested pier of cacophony, she scraped another car, or tractor, I'm not certain which, and I heard her call out "sorry" to someone and heard back a laughing guttural "no bother" – and off we went.

Steepest hill.

Family meal.

Loudest wash from sea.

Deepest sleep.

Perhaps a hypnopompic moment in the grand scheme of non-things.

Window open without worry.

Breakfast.

Jodie walked me to neighbour Mark's, teaching me my stickish way.

Mark.

Goats bleating in the shed out back.

Would goats get my goat?

"Hold out your hand," urged Mark half an hour later, initiation rite of cuppa done.

Slowly, tentatively, with a slight shake, I stuck out stick fingers.

"Easy now," he said. "It's safety first around here, what with no doctors about." He held my wrist. "They've only one set of teeth in front, so they can't bite you no matter what, well, not unless you get your hand too far back."

Mammy, where are you? Eve?

If a heart attack's coming, let it be now.

I held my breath, felt a soft bristly wet hardness. Then, with the tips of my fingers, the front teeth. And I thought, well, I've a second hand if he snatches this one off. But nothing happened. Well, nothing happening was something happening, nothing bad was something good.

I breathed.

The blind can lead the blind.

Thanks, mam.

Mark let go my wrist, stood beside me. And soon, I confess, I liked the very fact of handling the goats. When I touched one, I liked to touch them all, didn't like to show favourites. All fifteen of them. Even the kids got used to me and would nuzzle up. And they're intelligent. They may not talk, at least not our tongue, but they learn to understand phrases. I suspect they've their own Hermetic, know a lot of Trismegistus stuff we don't know they know. Mark once had a billy goat that escaped twice from his locked shed by sawing the door in half with his horny horns. Another used to pick the lock with its horn. And several ewes learned to slide the bolt back with their noses. Hearing these stories, I couldn't help thinking of the time Jimmy locked himself in my bathroom, all five or six years of him, and by the time I got Betsy's husband Tom to take the door off the hinges, Jimmy'd dumped everything from the medicine cabinet into the tub just because I told him he couldn't get in there. He made a flotilla out of my prescriptions, the scamp.

Yes, goats too could do well on IQ tests.

Goats the new world. Full of frolic. Soft. Affectionate. The opposite of imagined rhinoceri. Some, like Angelica, such a pet! Such a single row of royal ivory choppers. So gentle she let me clean the backs of 'em with scratches from my little finger. And tiny Rachael. And bony Christabel. Amiable souls all. But strange putting my hand into their feeding bowls and feeling their moist lips. That first time! Yes, time can stand still – even on my seventy-third birthday. I'd been afraid of horns, of being butted, of being bitten, so what for presents these touches of tongues, these nuzzles of nose. Thanks, Jimmy boy.

That afternoon, after milking, Mark asked if I'd ever tasted goat's milk. When I answered no, he touched my arm with a ladle full. I sipped from it a warm, fresh nectar. The texture rich, the smell pure. Made me think my milk in Cork thin, probably half water. Not a fair comparison.

At the end of my first day as a mature student of goats, while Mark cleaned up after the milking, I helped. I'd a little trouble undoing the clip that held each goat in her milking position. But then I discovered that the clip went from the stanchion to the goat rather than from the goat to the retaining rope. I said aloud, laughing, "I think Auntie Aggie's rather stupid." (But then, does the hand boast when it obeys the command of the heart?) And Mark, he started to laugh too. Both of us there, cleaning up, laughing and laughing. No wonder the Japanese have a saying I share with all priests, "Time spent laughing is time spent with god." We need to sneak that into the Gospel. I don't think King James would mind.

"By the end of the course," Mark brought me back from my laughter catharsis, "you'll know how to buy a goat, know a good one from a bad. While you can't learn to be a proficient milker in three days, you can get started. And develop a feel for individual animals. Which you're doing, Aggie."

So look out, Western Road, that's my pet billy goat, King Stinky himself, holding up traffic this rush hour Monday morning! Look both ways, and then some, when you cross in front of UCC and King Stinky.

Late that afternoon, I asked Mark about the problems of the blind teaching – not leading – the blind. He confessed he'd never thought of designing a course for the blind.

"I haven't had to make modifications for you, or next-to-none, Aggie. Except I have to be careful of my assumptions. Today, for example, when we practiced hoof trimming: Whenever I've taught people how to do this before, I've instructed them to hold the hoof up, whereas, when I'm alone, I face the hoof downwards since I don't need to see it. I forgot and told you to hold it up. Which made it more awkward for you. Several times I've said to you, 'It's over there,' forgetting to say it's to the left or right. See, I'm not used to living with a blind person! This whole thing about sight," he laughed, "isn't about sight but 3-D perception. You synthesise so much in your head. Why, it was easier for me to handle 3-dimensional geometry than for my sighted classmates."

On the second day, during an afternoon break, I asked Mark how he became enamoured of goats. "At the age of seven, blind for four years, I drank my first glass of goat's milk. Love at first taste. From a goat named Rosie. Scrumptious. Then, during university days, I'd a friend with goats and discovered they were a neglected species being squeezed out of agriculture. As an experiment, I kept a goat on the 190-acre campus, became connected to the goat, experienced goat as friend. But academic bureaucrats didn't take to my idea of starting a goat herd, doing away with many expensive gardeners, or using the milk in the cafeteria."

His story awoke in me a fantasy, that place where the mind goes into a different gear, where the engine makes a different noise. Not hyperborean but spindriftean. Maybe my Cork-based Goat Husbandry Centre could provide milk exclusively for the Mercy Hospital. Jimmy could prosper as my foreman when he retires from the army. Shifting grazing areas – front yard patches – would be no problem for him, what with his Hezbollah/Orthodox Jew experience. Patrick's Street for close grazing, the South Mall for kidding.

"Tell me, Mark, how'd you ever connect with Cape?" Me brazen?

"Later, when I'd become a lecturer in philosophy, I by chance vacationed on Cape – and dreamed of goats. So when I found a 33-acre farm for sale, I thought, maybe it's not insane to move here. I recognised the risk, knew that either you take it or you don't."

Like me now, having sold my Goat Husbandry Centre at an enormous profit, debating training seeing-eye goats, starting a whole new business for the unsighted. Can't you see me walking the length of Washington Street preceded by King Stinky, me an in-the-flesh advertisement that will revolutionise the way the blind navigate hill and dale, boulevard and avenue?

Slow down, Aggie. At your time in life you should be done with such day-dreaming. But is that really so, Hermes boy? Maybe at my time in life day-dreaming's even more important than when a child.

A whet stone for Mark's knife to smooth the hooves.

A kidney stone.

A goat stone.

An old as Methuselah's cat stone.

An omphalos foundation.

Home.

On my third day of being seventy-three, a neighbour of Mark's dropped by, an American blow-in into photography. After some chat, he said to me, "Since so much of my pleasure living here comes from a visual appreciation of ceaselessly changing, unspoilt nature, I wondered how your sense of this island compares to mine?"

"Why," I told this Fineen Hubbard, "Here's like another time, another place, another kind of existence. And the sound of the sea! I'm home." I skipped the omphalos but somewhat superstitiously placed my hand over my own navel.

Don't know if Fineen liked that answer, but he thanked me for sharing and left, saying he'd chores to do before the dance of evening light. And there I was having a fantasy of selling my Cork Goat Centre and with all the profits buying a farm on Cape. I'd then be in a position to found the world's first insane asylum for the blind off Ireland's south coast. Naturally the Ireish Tourist Board would do all my advertising free of charge.

See with what alacrity I can get off the island rabbit track? Cape makes me downright high. But I was after learning from Mark's goats. Mimesis, that's the stuff. Why, the moment I spot, or make, a weakness in the fence, I'm off to pastures new.

That third night Mark gave me a quote: "The goat must browse where she's tied." I answered him with a line from that eternity-in-a-grain-of-sand man: "The lust of the goat is the bounty of God."

Mark didn't come back at me. But then, the goat's usually been a symbol of Satan and black magic, so it's no wonder he's able to bring us up short once in awhile. Still, I guess, at least on this point, I'm in many ways more with the ancient Greeks: Baby Zeus suckled from a she-goat named Amalthea. Yes, back to the beginnings of things, no less than a goat for the mother of the king of the gods. (Tell that to your PP, you feral iconoclast.) Why, even our closer neighbour Thor had his chariot harnessed to a gaggle of goats as he zipped about the heavens. I digress from my digression in my ecstasy.

But then, Mark really does fly around the place. Hard work. And such a standard of hygiene in the milking parlour. Scrub scrub scrub a dub dub. And his down-to-earth work reminded me that miracles – like being able to see of a sudden – are for those of little faith.

That reminds me of what was most difficult about the course proper. Milking. I never could get much. Just not the knack. The pressure of the hand determines how goats sense inexperience. I did get a little milk from Christabel, the one whose hip bones stick up more. Mark told me that I did reasonably well. Average or above even. "Like all manual skills," he said, "you learn by extended experience how hard to squeeze. You don't use those muscles much." I didn't tell him that arthritis in my index and middle fingers might have been a hindrance.

And so my course on Cape came to an end. Or a beginning. The island clarified for this pernickety old audio book babe out of arms that what you don't get by your own work isn't yours. No one can touch a goat for you. No one can tappety tap tap tap down the lane without a verge for you. Anymore than anyone can breathe for you.

Another stone.

Not enough? Or too much? So old Billy Boy Blake condenses all chances at life.

And Mark? Direct as the sun, as full of ideas as the Milky Way of stars. Which reminds me: If I could see for just a second in my whole life, I'd like to witness the nighttime sky of light-free Cape. I can feel a face, or a leaf, or a goat, but a star, a constellation . . . an emptiness of mind.

Then that blow-in bit of birdsong, that Fineen, dropped in again on my last day, after the course ended. Came by and took me for a walk, right out to the edge of some cliffs – not someplace I could've gone alone or with Mark. With his hand onto my flop, he guided me along narrow rabbit tracks that turned and twisted every couple of feet. Six inches wide. One foot in front of t'other. Short steps. And he walking through bracken and the prickliest of perfumed gorse, no bother, he there for me every step of the way. Me both handmaid and queen, that track the red carpet treatment. Finally he sat me down on the comfiest, most hummocky of grass – and we listened. Didn't talk, didn't have to. Surrounded by the sound of the sea, the loudness of a vast silence. We sat and we sat. And the silence, it rose up and up like that tidal wave, and then carried me down and down and down. And deposited me on the most solid Earth I've ever felt. That sea silence a symphony, Mozart's posthumous prelude to his Fiftieth, complete with trident, whelk, and porpoise.

Three spaces of time.

The loudness of vast silence.

A little later, an hour or a year, we got to chatting. He eventually asked me a direct question, you know, about things that happened back in my dark and middle ages. I suddenly remembered learning to play the harp in a primary-level boarding school for the blind. Some angel, huh? And right after secondary school, I guess I fell, told him, for instead of learning to fly I trained as a telephonist. Me in my early twenties. Worked a large board – a PBX, sorry, a Private Branch Exchange – with 50 numbers, both for my above-mentioned friend, the ESB, and for our beloved Mercy. Those were the days, my friend, before Bob Dylan, when giving somebody a plug – making connections too! – was what I was all about! Now I see it's not so easy to get such jobs because of automation. Thank goodness I was able to retire – twelve years ago already – before this high-tech revolution.

I even told him about my teens and early twenties, they my most difficult period. Boy friends. Trying to decipher a soul from the feel of a face. Awkward. That may not hold for everybody. From all I heard from my sister, bless her, it certainly didn't for her. But it tended to make me shy. Though I certainly wasn't unhappy, or not all the time. I joined a club for the blind, took up a white stick, slow and tedious – and sure. I still don't know if I should have married, or become a nun, or specialised in getting off the beaten track. But nothing ever moved me, pushed me hard enough. Maybe as a compensation for my blindness I grew too thick a skin. So be it. That was then. This is now. My boobs may dangle waistline empty, bellybutton between 'em, but the pump beneath their base is full. Albeit with a matronly trickle of schmaltz.

Sitting in that silence with Fineen reminded me that that person who hasn't a single hour for him- or herself on a daily basis can't be human.

Ouch. I just bit pompous Aggie's tongue.

When Fineen returned me to Jodie's, he thanked me for my company. I couldn't say a word but held out me hand. When he took it we hugged. Fifty years too late my foot.

So you see, a gift doth blind the eyes of the wise and pervert the wisdom of the ages. Yes, we should just be like an old jug that happily receives whatever its owner dumps into it, whether wine or vinegar, Guinness or Cork's Murphy's – or goat's milk. We can't outlaw catastrophe. A tidal wave sweeps in and carries off every island house. But I'm seventy-three. There are now no tragedies that can happen directly to me. Suffering, sure; tragedy no. I may never have twigged on to the colour difference between lilac and cinnamon, but the wild blue black yonder's now my friend. Yes yes, I've recently placed my hand in the wild goat's mouth – and lived to tell this tale. When you follow a goat – or a rabbit, a Fineen – you get off the beaten track. Even tappety tap tap tap's not enough. Why, maybe this rambling account, and Cape itself, are but feral goats in another form. Am I moving into eternity as I milk these metaphoric creatures?

And you, dear reader, you may have noticed I haven't yet mentioned Christ, not even once . . . until now. Though Mozart's pretty close. Anyway, pardon me. But I'm thinking, 'cause it's bedtime now and time for me to stop thinking, that, no matter how much wisdom we can learn, whether from goats or roads or peaceful places, since I'm going to be a farmer, I've got to add that to be true to my stubborn stickish septuagenarian self, I mustn't see Him as the Messiah, but as a ploughman who calls out to his horse, Giddy-up, giddy-up. Go widdershins 'round that omphalos.

Anchors Aweigh

Mags could not believe the amount of death around her. Cousin Bob drowned at sea, all twenty-seven years of him; Maura left behind to raise the twins. Sweet neighbour Sean gone at forty after a three-year struggle with cancer; lost his battle but never his smile. And friend and mentor Padraig. About to celebrate his seventy-fifth it's true, but she didn't expect someone to go out shopping for a new trailer hitch for his tractor and not come home. Just like that. All in the past three months. And last week, at long last, her poor wisp of a mother suffering from a second bout with lung cancer – her right lung removed five years ago – finally gave up the ghost.

She knew she had to take action, but what action? She didn't want to mope, stay or become depressed – she wasn't certain where she was – but she also didn't know how to break out of the cocoon of death around her. While she easily recognised that without death life would have no meaning, that seemed a philosophical perspective that had nothing immediate to do with her.

And then a recent memory started to awaken in her. At her mother's funeral, Micheál, a UCC professor friend, had shared his condolences.

"Mags, forgive me, but what I want to say comes from what helped me through my parents' deaths. You might not have heard of him – I haven't yet met any student of mine who has – but there's a Japanese poet name Kenji Miyazawa, and he suggests that we embrace pain, burn it as a fuel on our journey. And I believe that if we do, pain can become deeply social, shareable, despite the increasing tendency of our culture to cover it up and bury it under a rug in the parlour. Put pain to good use in your own life."

Yes, girl, now's the time to start burning the fuel. But how do I light it?

She looked around her. With her youngest twenty-one, and all three off, all working into careers rather than just jobs, they were no longer where she could or should give herself – unless they needed her. And maybe now they needed her not to be around. Husband Charlie, he was there for her, and she for him, and this relationship she felt as lucky and complete as any could be. She could see no way in which their connection needed any major change. Her garden? Big enough to give them something fresh every day of the year. Even now, in the salt-washed dead of winter gale season, she was still picking purple sprouting broccoli, spinach, rosemary, and the last of the summer cabbage. And she liked the image of doing more work outside, of stepping into the wind, digging spade into the earth, for otherwise she'd end up being – before she ended being altogether – compost, simply something to decompose and be dug under. Here she felt herself let loose an insouciant inner grin. What was it Meister Eckhard once wrote? She tugged on memory as if it were a bell rope. And she heard the clang, clang reverberate above garden beds: "Every creature is a word of God." So move it, girl. Put your pain to work.

Over morning tea with Charlie, she shared.

"You need something new, yes. Not that your poor mother can ever be replaced, God bless her. But you're not telling me that all you do around this little farm bores you?" he responded. "I mean, we're rich. We've the grass of a goat and a cow."

"You and your mother. Wish she could see us now with our hundred forty acres and a mischievous herd of pedigree Kerries. And all tucked down beside and above the sea. But then, maybe all our parents are watching us right now."

They looked out the kitchen window, across two pastures and on to a light-puddled sea.

"Well? What is it? You want some 13-hand ponies, old-style Connemaras? Want some saddleback pigs? Want to go to art school or study medicine? Start a business? Want to run an animal farm for children now that your mother doesn't need your help?"

"Charlie."

"More work for the Red Cross, Amnesty International?"

"Yes, that's closer to it. But hands-on work. Not writing letters to presidents about prisoners in Guantánamo, the indictment of justice on an international scale; not taking more refresher courses in first aid, but –"

"But nothing. How 'bout that, sweetheart?"

Charlie pointed to the far point, an RNLI lifeboat rounding the stack. As they watched the craft power along, a second lifeboat came into view. In all their years together – they'd been married for twenty-six – they'd never before seen two lifeboats at once on what was apparently a coastal practice run, not a rescue mission.

"Maybe you're spot on, Charlie," said Mags, as she stood, walked around the kitchen table, and, from behind, threw her arms around him, pressed her substantial starting-to-sag warm breasts into his shoulder blades, leaned her head and neck around him, kissed him under his chin, on his Adam's apple, and, lingeringly, on the hollow at the top of his throat. He tilted his head backwards, reached his arms behind him, hugged the backs of her thighs.

"Ah, what a dewlap," she whispered, tears wetting her cheeks.

"Ah, what a gaskin yourself," he said warmly, comfortingly.

"Those two, they must be Castletownbere and Courtmac making a joint manoeuver. Sure but Baltimore's Tyne Class isn't up to that size. Charlie, I'm going to take your tip, and the advice of Micheál: go see the cox right now, assuming Johnny's not out there, and see if there's space for a forty-five-year-old grieving matron amongst the volunteers."

"A first."

"A synchronicity."

"A whatever-you-say, Miss Education."

"I'm off. Not to see the wizard but the world of energy-burning men. Mam always spoke highly of the RNLI. 10:43. I'll time how long it takes to zip from Ballymacrown to the lifeboat station. Slán."

Mags kissed the centre of his balding head – and dashed off, into her mother's ten-year-old black VW beetle, down the mile-long dirt road, dust swirling behind her, until she reached the outskirts of Baltimore, where she turned left onto the main road, then right, and the quarter mile to the lifeboat station. 10.48. Seconds under five minutes. She knew – if accepted as a volunteer – she could make the run in the requisite time.

A shadow fell over her. She looked out the window . . . and up. Daniel, the lifeboat mechanic – the only salaried member of the crew

– had come out to see who was there. She opened her door.

"Hello, Daniel. How are you?" When he merely nodded, she quickly swung her legs out, stood, moved outside his shadow. "Would Johnny be about?"

"Why do you ask?" he replied somewhat gruffly. And then, remembering, he added, "And sorry I am to hear about your mother."

"Thank you. Yes, she's partly why I'm here, in fact. And why I want to see Johnny. I've an idea I want to bounce off him. Is he here?"

"Were there an emergency, he'd be here. But right now, and usually, as I thought you knew, he's running the store. What's this all about, Mags? I saw you drive up, hit the brakes, check your watch the second you stopped. Now I've seen many a man do the same, but nary a woman. And now you want Johnny."

"Yes. I've had a thought. I'd like to become a volunteer."

"A volunteer?"

"A volunteer."

"We don't have any women crew, Mags. Can't be done, twenty-first century or not."

"Just what I thought. So it's time."

"Time for you to help us raise money, or manage the books, or locate a good profile for a fundraising event, sure, but on board, no way."

"Is that final?"

"Look, Mags, I'm not against women or anything, but the sea's no place for a tea party. To bring off these rescues, we need muscle, brawn –"

"Thanks, Daniel. I'm off to talk with Johnny – and not about any sex change or MCP prejudice," she said, climbing back into the beetle.

"I'll give him a ring on my mobile, let him know."

"Fore-warned's four-armed, mam used to say, but who wants to be half an octopus. Bye."

Daniel spun on his heel, reentered the station.

Mags sat at the wheel, trembling. She felt as if she'd run her mother's car off the road at the foot of Hungry Hill, West Cork's highest mountain, and straight away rammed against base of sheer cliff. So what to do? she asked herself. Back up, girl; get going again on the real road, not the road of your imagination. Sure there'll be switchbacks, detours, dead ends, and so what. On with it, Mags. Make your mam proud of you. Put her death to good use. Hum up!

She drove off from the station, followed the harbour road past a dilapidated shipyard, two minutes later parked at the foot of the main pier in the small heart of Baltimore, but a heart, she thought that, come summer, and yachties, sailing schools, seafood festivals, antique boat races, beats with the rapidity of a Big Smoke hub. If there aren't too many deaths.

"Over here, Mags!" There he was, the cox waiting for her at the top of the boatyard steps. They shook hands, he gently patting her shoulder, his eyes full of condolence, his head nodding.

"Hi, Johnny. Thanks, yes. She's better off. Out of all that pain."

"My mamaí always said 'souls grow by subtraction'."

"I'll remember that. In fact, I like it so much could we just be quiet with that thought for a bit, and then get down to business?"

"Be quiet away."

Mags shut her eyes for a minute. Johnny waited, and when he saw her eyes open, he said, "Anyway, been expecting you."

"That quick, was he, that Daniel."

"Oh, I've been expecting you for years. Sit down. Here." He patted a stone step. "We need to chat."

"He briefed you?"

"He did."

"And you'll still talk to me?"

"Don't judge a book by first reviews. We've a pretty standard procedure, and we'll put you to the test we apply to all volunteers. Daniel's a little put off, maybe partly because three women have tried to become members recently, and none has passed the test, but you, you might be the first exception. You've the sea in your blood. I remember your grandfather Teddy, he used to sell fish to my grandfather, and your four uncles, they were all active RNLI volunteers. So why not you? And I know you've done some professional nursing, too. What am I missing?"

"Well," she replied, finally sitting beside him on the step, "first thing in the morning, as a youngster, I'd go for a swim if the tide was in, dive down to where I'd collect periwinkles and build rock castles at low tide. Older, I'd drive my brothers over to the emergency calls, wave them off into the adventurous unknown."

"And now you want some of that for yourself?"

"Yeah, now I want to put myself in a different harness, see what it's like to pull a plough at sea."

"You can be gone from home for 30 hours at a stretch?"

"If necessary."

"And where's Charlie on all this?"

"Behind me," she smiled, remembering his last hug. "Behind me all the way."

"OK, Mags. Look," he said, reaching into his coat pocket, "here's the new form to fill out. Get yourself a medical exam, not just a check-up, but a physical and mental exam, with eyesight tested –a colour-blindness check too – for us to send to England. Be at the station by 2:00 p.m. this Saturday for a practice run. We'll go – unless we're already out on call. Every two weeks. A year's probation. If all goes well, you're in like Flynn. What think you?"

"Thanks, Johnny."

"No bother. I probably ought to tell you that in-house training used to be enough. Not no more. Now you've got to be signed off by outside experts on first aid, VHF, radio protocol, engine maintenance, navigation, etcetera, etcetera. But don't be after worrying about all that. Start with becoming expert at putting on our new lifejacket. Yes, even that. What with all the insurance and litigation problems nowadays, putting on a lifejacket just right's no joke. Then throwing anchors, pyrotechnics, how to fire a flare. Here."

He handed her the preliminary form.

They stood, shook hands as if sealing a bargain.

As they walked off in opposite directions, Mags called back to him, "And I'll work on that subtraction."

On the way home she found herself wondering what kind of gardener Daniel would be. Not organic. He wouldn't be into butterfly bushes but pesticides. She caught herself. Not fair. That's adding to the soul, not subtracting. Daniel too's a word of God. But I don't want to hear you say so. Who's you? My math teacher?

On Saturday Mags arrived at 1:45. Aidan, a twenty-two-year-old whose father ran the local diving school and who was on his eleventh practice run, helped her select her gear, showed her how to work the lifejacket, complete with flare and whistle, where to mount the spiraling metal stairs up to the *Hilda Jarrett*, which waited secure at the top of the slipway. Looking up at it, she thought of a spaceship with her mother aboard.

"We blast off, I mean shoot down that slipway, ker-splash, and power away, no?"

"Oh, it's a ride down, Mags. A sliding board for adults. You want to hang on – and be ready for the power take-off when we hit the drink. You don't need to clip your lifejacket to no jackwire, but hold on tight."

She felt as if she wanted to hold on just looking at the lifeboat. While used to the orange cabin and the blue hull above the waterline, she'd never seen the lower part of the hull before, a glistening polished white mass looming above her head, nor had she ever before stood beside the brass propellers. She imagined the lifeboat at the top of the slipway as if it were some giant's arrow about to be released.

Mags climbed the stairs, walked to the open side of the station – where the *Hilda Jarrett*'s bow jutted out into the fresh air – and looked about. The slipway sloped some sixty feet down to the sea. In the harbour she focused on a ro-ro – a hundred-fifty-foot of roll-on roll-off barge – moored five hundred yards northeast, the island of Ringarogy straight ahead, Sherkin Island and the Franciscan Abbey ruins to the south. Somewhere behind her and out of sight her farm, her garden, her dependable husband Charlie, her –

"All aboard," Johnny shouted. Seconds later engines roared. Through the scramble of kitting up, Mags rushed back, reached for stanchion, pulled herself aboard without assistance from proffered hand. The men, some still with lifejacket toggles dangling at their feet, gathered aft of the main cabin, though Daniel, Mags quickly noted, was sitting downstairs at the second helm, the mechanic's helm. Johnny commanded its sister wheel on the back of the forecabin.

As Mags whispered goodbye to the Charlie in her mind, they were off. A cog system lowered them halfway down the shoot, then released them. To Mags they had been not jettisoned but fired toward the sea. She held her breath. White bow splash whipped overhead. And at moment of impact Johnny gunned the vessel. Mags felt herself pushed against the closed aft compartments, containers, whatever they were, she wasn't certain. This was no winter wind coating her broccoli with salt and sea spit.

She turned around. Stern wake rose like a geyser, gradually flattened out. They purred through December seas. She could be sitting before their fireplace with cat in lap. Mags felt herself start to breathe again as the forty-seven foot, twenty-six ton steel-hulled self-righting lifeboat – she'd memorised the details from the RNLI website – was, within seconds of take-off, relaxedly cruising at top speed of eighteen knots. She grinned as the thought occurred to her that no John Deere could plough this fast.

Half an hour later, in easy, two-metre swells, Johnny signalled to Daniel to bring the Hilda Jarrett to a halt and keep her steady, bow into the thrust of a hundred-metre-wide 3-knot rip-tide that crackled round them, heading west, while he walked forward, stood with back against bow post cum pulpit. The seven in training – five men in their late teens to early twenties, another in his mid-forties, and Mags – gathered before him.

Mags remembered her catechism classes and how they'd group before Father Dan, her mother's favourite priest.

"What's the tide up to?" asked Johnny.

"Going out," offered Colum, a local fisherman. "And, as the finger-nail moon up there tells, it's a late spring."

"How many of you" – Johnny unzipped a pocket, pulled out a tiny blue booklet – "have a tide table on you?"

Three, including Mags, shook their heads. She liked the size of this bible. And so incontrovertible. God at her best as reported by man.

"From now on, a must. At all times. Available at every pub in town. Now why's it essential to know the tides?"

"Well, if we're trying to rescue some capsized sailors in this rip," said Mags, wishing Father Dan could hear, "we'd have to take the current – and not just the swells – into consideration."

"Where it's safe to go at high tide, we could run aground at low," added Aidan.

Father Dan, she thought, even Eden isn't all it's cracked up to be.

"What's going on over there?" asked Johnny, pointing to a stretch of dark water a quarter mile south.

"Tide colliding with itself," answered Colum. "Its flow swoops around a reef and then crashes into itself on the far side. Messy. A lot more so when it swoops around an island, then collides afterwards in a narrow stretch like the Gaisceanán. What might be heavy swells elsewhere become cliffs where tidal flows meet. And I mean all but vertical mountains of water."

Noah – she caught herself asking – with all those words of God aboard, did you ever see or hear the likes of this? And what did you use for fuel?

"Right. And we've pulled off a few operations in those very waters. Just two years ago that's where the *Dina* went down. We got all eight aboard, and she sank within a minute of the last rescue. Anyway, lads," – he gave Mags an inclusive wink – "knowing the tides, what's here right now, what's to happen in the next hour, that can make a critical difference to a rescue operation.

"And now, lads, time to go to work. Mags, you first. Time to learn to shoot and haul anchor in a rip. And no sea-anchor or drogue this baby. She'll catch if you learn to give her just the right amount of slack once she hits bottom. Then the heavy stock lies flat and positions one of the flukes to be ready to dig in when the drag begins. Anyway, after this exercise, we'll relax, go round the Fastnet, head for home. Watch close now."

And watch close Mags did. She saw herself in an alternative new garden learning how to double-dig beds of sea bottom for her energy plants.

Johnny signalled Daniel to shift into neutral as he released the safety catch on the anchor rope. Lifting the sixty-pound anchor by gravity band and top of shank, he walked it to the very bow, pitched it slightly to starboard, rope snaking out of its below-deck coil, Johnny standing clear should there be any hitch. When anchor hit bottom, Johnny quickly paid out extra rope to let shank and stock lie down, and then, as the boat drifted in the rip, gave a series of little tugs until a fluke snagged. When sufficiently proven that the anchor was holding, despite waves, rip, and pull of boat, he signaled to Daniel to motor forward. When bow was directly above anchor, he motioned to Daniel to hold her there and gave a series of quick tugs, freed the embedded fluke, hand over hand raised anchor. Once ring reached rub rail, he leaned over, lifted the anchor aboard, motioned to Mags.

Called, girl. Before the entire congregation. With Satan down below and waiting for sin of mistake. Burn, baby, burn!

Scared but determined, she stepped forward, checked that the rope was carefully coiled. Just before she tried to heft the anchor from where Johnny had left it, she signaled through the cabin window to Daniel to shift into neutral so that the boat would drift away from where she'd drop anchor. She then lifted the anchor, fully aware that it was essential for her to heft it with legs rather than back. With shank against left hip, she stepped to gunwale, then hesitated, as Daniel Satan bugger-boy hadn't eased off on throttle. Struggling to balance shank on bent left thigh, and thoughts of right brain, she twisted toward Daniel, again gave the cut signal.

In the beginning was the gesture, and the gesture was nobody.

Seconds seemed light years.

Daniel shifted.

Mags straightened up. Heaved the anchor out. Jumped back from uncoiling rope. When its speed suddenly diminished, she picked up rope and gave requisite tugs. All went as with Johnny, including the last signal to Daniel to hold the boat steady once the anchor was straight below.

Fallen angels can learn to fly, Mam.

When she'd finished hoisting anchor to rub rail, heart pounding, and then lifting it up and up, again onto her left thigh, face turning bright red, she felt, while returning anchor to its place, as if she'd just given birth, an Eve to an Abel. With God for a Grandmother. She knew her body was covered in drippy sweat, especially the back of her neck, her shoulders, her armpits, her crotch. But she could now relax. And the lads, who'd already neatly coiled the rope, preparatory to the next heave, congratulated her.

Mags grinned at the crew as she privately imagined Abel sucking at her breast, his Grandmother smiling. Aren't we all archetypes at times. Her grin filled her world.

Anchor practice over, the Fastnet Lighthouse rounded, Mags climbed into the forecabin, walked up beside Daniel and quietly watched him steer. Finally she chanced, "What's it like, Daniel, to pilot this baby."

Not Abel, girl; don't get confused.

He turned toward her, stood, said, "Here, take the wheel, Mags. Find out for yourself. I'm no good at explaining things. Head straight for the Catalogue Islands, with Turk's Head pier behind 'em. I'll be back in a bit. But first I've got to share a secret: you just passed the very test three other women failed. The primary physical test. Didn't think a woman could do it. Congrats."

Daniel Satan new friend walked aft and outside, leaving Mags at the gift of helm and alone with her thoughts. She checked the wheel's responsiveness, realised that the slightest movement on her part had immediate effect. When she spotted a lobster buoy a hundred yards off, straight ahead, she veered west, returned to course.

Imagine piloting a universe. And how many universes are there out there that this radar system doesn't show? Could our universe be like that buoy in the system of things? Ahoy, girl. Come back down to this earth, this sea. Could death, properly handled, be like an anchor?

Two miles later, Daniel returned, stood beside her, answered questions about how much fuel the engine had burnt today, taught her how to work the throttle as they entered Baltimore Harbour. She felt as if she were parachuting back down to earth and realised it was time to start cooking dinner.

Two years later, at the annual Baltimore RNLI fund-raising dinner dance in the Beacon Park Hotel, with Charlie by her side, Mags was asked to come forward. "During a rescue operation this last winter, a truly desperate dirty shout," Johnny recounted to the crowd, "Mags somehow spotted a body face down in the midnight chop – lumpy waters the rest of us had scanned to no avail. At her direction, Aidan jumped in, pulled the body to the lifeboat. As we hauled him aboard, Nurse Mags went straight to work, succeeded in the mouth-to-mouth resuscitation manoeuver that brought our local fisherman Ger O'Toole back to life. Ger would now like to present this RNLI plaque to Mags."

As Mags stood, she felt Charlie's hand discreetly give a little pat to the back of her calf. Amid the applause he whispered, "Well done, you old sea dog! Your mother'd be proud of you too!"

"What mother?" Mags whispered back. "She's free of me now."

"Mags," Johnny said, "would you please step up here and say a few words."

He handed her the microphone.

"Very briefly, I'd just like to say thanks to all who support the RNLI and that what I did wasn't done by me but by all of us. What a privilege for us all to be able to help a life go on. God bless. She's good at it."